THE
YOUNGEST
PATRIOT

To Helen and Lae
dear and special friends
Irene

THE
YOUNGEST
PATRIOT

---

*The Story of the British
Occupation of Long Island*

Gene Ligotti

[signature]

7/29/2000

78-LiGO

To order additional copies of this book, contact:
Xlibris Corporation
1-888-7-XLIBRIS
www.Xlibris.com
Orders@Xlibris.com

CONTENTS

This book, as is my life,
is dedicated to my wife,
Corbina,
without whom neither would have
purpose or meaning

78-LIGO

ONE

Children cheered and ran through the streets. Shopkeepers, who would normally tend to their business, stepped outside their stores to get a better look at him. This was his town. He was born here and until a few years ago this town was his whole world. He rode through the small village of Setauket waving to all the people he knew, and he knew them all. They had seen him ride through the village on horseback many times before without turning a head, let alone gathering a crowd, but this time it was different. It was not the horse, although this highly spirited animal pranced and held his head high as if he had caused the commotion. This time, Benjamin Tallmadge was in uniform, and what a splendid uniform it was. Although in June of 1776 uniforms were new to the people, it was obvious to all, that this tall handsome young man, with angular features and an out thrust jaw, was an officer. His bright blue coat was faced with white. The blue cloak of an officer, which he wore over his right shoulder, fluttered and flapped as he rode. The bright afternoon sun caused flashes of gleaming light to bounce off the buttons of his jacket and the sword in its scabbard. The stallion's coat glistened with an iridescent black sheen. Benjamin's metal helmet, trimmed in silver, was topped with beautiful white horsehair plumes flowing from its peak. Yes, from the magnificent gallant snow-white plumes to his highly polished black cavalry boots, this handsome man was indeed an officer. His patrician features gave him the natural look of breeding and culture. He was a Lieutenant in the Second Regiment of Light Dragoons.

Others in Setauket had joined General Washington's young Continental Army. From all of Long Island they had come, to do their part to drive the English out. Benjamin was different, and not just because he was an officer. He had graduated from Yale college three years ago and was a high school principal at the young age of twenty-two. The proud townspeople cheered for Benjamin and for their fledgling country, proud of its fine young men who were giving up so much to fight for a righteous cause.

Benjamin spurred his horse onward and although the children tried to keep up with him he easily outdistanced them. With a final wave, to his friends and neighbors with his plumed helmet, he turned his steed off the main street and headed southward toward Brookhaven and his father's farm. He slowed his horse to a walk and enjoyed one of the many tree shaded lanes which turned lazily off the main street of the usually sleepy town. After being away for so long, he would have liked to have revisited more of the town's main street, but he was embarrassed over the excitement he had stirred up.

Benjamin deliberately chose this particular road for his 'escape' from the townspeople, in hopes that Mary Floyd might just see him as he rode by. Mary was a girl that Benjamin had been fond of when he was about fourteen years old. To his knowledge, she had not shared his feelings of affection. As he passed her house, people he did not recognize waved to him from the front porch. He acknowledged their friendly greeting with a smile and a slight bow of the head. Perhaps the Floyd family had moved. As he traveled down the road and beyond the homes into the countryside he continued to think about Mary. He thought about his little fantasy; that perhaps she would see him and the uniform would make a difference. He laughed aloud at the wonder of puppy love and how the years had not dulled its intrigue.

"Do you find me amusing, sir?" came a voice from behind him.

Benjamin was startled. He turned to see a young boy, of about fourteen or so, mounted on a mule approaching him. He smiled at the boy, noticing how different they were now and how alike they would have been when he was the same age.

"I was not laughing at you. In truth, I had not seen you approach. It was a private matter which struck my fancy and caused me to laugh. I assure you, my laughter was not directed at you," said Benjamin.

"Then please forgive my rudeness, sir. My name is Elijah, Elijah Churchill. My father has a small farm nearby"

"My father also has farmland not far from here and it's he who I come to visit today. It'll be quite a surprise for him since he doesn't know that I'm coming and doesn't know about this," said Benjamin flourishing with his hand at his new uniform.

"Oh, how I wish that I had a uniform, . . . that is, if I was able to enlist, but my father is against it. He says that the cause is right, but he feels that I'm too young."

"The army would agree with him, Elijah," said Benjamin as he moved his horse closer to the mule and the fair-haired boy.

"Is it my fault that I am young? I want to take part in this great adventure. It's the beginning of a whole new country. The future will look back on this time with pride and if I don't do something it'll all pass and I'll have missed my chance to be part of it. All because I'm too young?"

"Elijah, you're a fine young man and you speak as one with more years than your —"

"I'm thirteen, but I look much older, sir. I'm sorry, sir, but I don't know your name."

"An oversight on my part. I am Lieutenant Benjamin Tallmadge of the Second Regiment Light Dragoons. It's a Connecticut regiment."

"Why a regiment from Connecticut if you live here?"

"I was a teacher and principal at a high school in Weathersfield, Connecticut, where I now make my home. I'm here only to visit my father and then I must report to regiment headquarters in New York."

"Take me with you, Lieutenant Tallmadge. Please take me with you!" said a very excited Elijah.

"I cannot. You really are too young and doesn't your father need you on his farm?"

"I do help my father, but he can manage very well without

me. Please, won't you reconsider? I'll do anything. Isn't an officer allowed to have a groom or a helper of some sort?"

"Perhaps you mean a valet. Yes, but I'm not a high ranking officer and besides, you seem to have the idea that life in the army is all glory. There's more to war than just uniforms. I'm sorry, Elijah, you'll have to wait until you are older."

Elijah didn't smile. He was crushed. Benjamin continued, "When you are older, I'm sure that the army will accept you. Until then, I wish you well." Benjamin Tallmadge offered his hand to the boy. Elijah's facial expression was one of complete rejection. He hung his head and took Benjamin's hand.

They shook hands in silence and Benjamin galloped off down the road. Elijah turned the mule in the opposite direction and started off. After only a few yards he stopped and stared off in the direction Tallmadge had taken. With a sparkle in his eye, he again turned his mule and followed the disappearing horseman.

Benjamin Tallmadge Sr. pulled his team of mules to a halt and stepped away from the plow blade. Taking a handkerchief from his pocket, he mopped his brow and squinted across the hot, newly plowed field at a lone rider approaching the farm. At first the rider appeared to be very tall, taller than most men. No, that's some sort of a hat he is wearing, thought the thin middle-aged man. Yes, it's a hat or a helmet. Why, it's a soldier.

Benjamin's father rubbed his eyes to help clear his vision and moved toward the rider, who now looked somehow familiar to him. But no, it couldn't be. "Oh, my God, it is!" he said aloud.

"Benjamin, Benjamin my son," he said. The elated man ran toward the galloping horse.

"Father," yelled Benjamin, dismounting as the horse drew close to his father, not waiting for the animal to come to a stop. He pushed off the horse, almost as if he felt he could run faster, and ran to embrace his father.

They held each other tightly for a moment and then separated. Smiling, continually looking at and circling one another, they embraced once again.

"So good to see you," they both said in unison and then laughed.

"When did all this happen?" said the elder Tallmadge, pointing at Benjamin's uniform.

"Father, I have so much to tell you."

"Come into the house. We'll get something cool to drink and have something to eat. Are you hungry, boy?"

They unhooked the mules from the plow and walked them, along with Benjamin's horse, into the barn. Neither of them noticed a young boy slide off an old mule by a shaded clump of trees near the Tallmadge farmhouse.

It was cooler in the house, but nevertheless, Benjamin removed his cloak and jacket and placed them over a chair. As he removed his sword, scabbard and belt, his father remarked, "You're an officer."

"Yes, father, I am. They felt that with my education and my position as a principal, I should be an officer."

Benjamin looked about the farmhouse that he had not seen for over a year. His father was a widower and the pastor at the Setauket Presbyterian Church. It pleased Benjamin that there had been no changes in the farmhouse. Everything was exactly as he had remembered.

"I'm proud that you are an officer, but you know that I was, and still am, against this whole mess. I don't want you in the army."

"I wish that I could understand you, father. You're in favor of the revolution, I know you are, and yet you are reluctant to see me in uniform. If every father felt as you do, who would fight this revolution that you so favor?

"Your brother for one," he answered with a far off look in his eyes.

"Will joined the army as well? How wonderful! When did he go? Where did he report?"

"William left two weeks ago for New York. I don't remember the regiment. Now both my sons will be in this war against the British. Will either of you ever return to me? You're all I have since your mother passed away." He stood and walked to the window somehow lost in thought.

"Without freedom none of us will ever have anything. Without freedom life is not worth living."

"I know that, boy, didn't I say that I was proud of you?" said the senior Tallmadge, annoyed that he had to be reminded of his steadfast beliefs.

Benjamin and his father talked for a long time. Each trying not to discuss the revolution or the army. Benjamin had questions about the farm and the town. He asked about old friends and what had become of them. Mary Floyd and her family had moved as Benjamin had suspected, north across the Long Island Sound to either Connecticut or Massachusetts.

"What ever happened to that Hale boy, you know, the one who you met when you were both students at Yale?"

"Nathan? He joined the army too. He's quartered in Connecticut. I tried to talk him out of enlisting, but he did, oh, it must be a year ago. I write to him often. He's not very well, and is extremely anxious over the fact that he has not done anything noteworthy to help the cause of our revolution."

"You try to dissuade your friends, but still you enlisted!"

"Father . . . "

The elder Benjamin raised his hand in a gesture that showed his son that he didn't expect or want an answer. After a few minutes of silence the father continued. "When next you write to young Mr. Hale, give him my greetings. Will you do that for me, son?"

"Yes, Father, I will."

"How long can you stay with me? When must you report?"

"I'll leave in the morning, very early," said Benjamin.

"I'll wake early as well, so we can make our farewells."

"Father, there's no need for you to . . . "

"I'll wake early so that we can make our farewells," repeated his insistent father.

"Yes, Father, I'd like that."

Elijah Churchill had been listening outside the window during almost all of the conversation between the two men. When he knew the time that Lieutenant Tallmadge was going to take his leave, he crept back to his mule, mounted the animal and quickly rode off toward his home.

*

Elijah was quiet during the supper hour, and although his brother and sister kept up a run-on conversation, his silence did not go unnoticed by his mother or his father.

Bringing food to the table, his mother passed close to her older son and pressed the back of her hand against his forehead.

"Are you well, Elijah?"

"Yes, Mother, why do you ask?"

"Well, you're not your usual talkative self."

"Oh, I'm fine. May I have more of the stew, please?"

"Where were you today? I could have used your help," asked his father angrily as he passed the bowl of stew to his son.

"I went into town . . . "

"Did you see the officer with the beautiful uniform?" interrupted his six year old sister, Betsy.

Elijah's younger brother chimed in at well. "The whole town is talking about him. There's going to be a war, isn't there, Father? We'll finally drive the Redcoats out. Isn't that right, Father?"

Elijah's father waved his youngest son into silence and once again spoke to Elijah. "What did you do in town, boy?"

Elijah looked up from his food as his feelings exploded from him. "Father, if you only could have seen him and talked to him. Our revolution, this war with the British, will bring about a new nation, a whole new country. We'll be free and independent."

The silence that followed Elijah's outburst was unexpected. He knew his father's thoughts on the subject of war and couldn't understand his silence. He expected a heated eruption of angry words. Elijah continued to eat but stole quick glances at his father, who simply refused to discuss the matter. Elijah could see by his

father's facial expression that he was not at all pleased. Not wanting to become involved, Elijah's mother busied herself with the dishes.
His brother and sister knew that it was best not to talk at all.

"Father, I . . . " Elijah started to speak but an angry glance
from his father stifled his words. He finished his supper, excused
himself from the table, and went outside to start his evening chores.

In the barn, he tried to think of the best way to express his
feelings to his father. Although in his mind the decision was already made as to what he would do, he still preferred to have his
father's permission. He thought of talking to his mother first, but
quickly dismissed that idea. His mother couldn't give him the
blessing he wanted and she might forbid him from any discussion
with his father. There was no use in antagonizing both his parents.

Later that evening, when the fire was reduced to just a flicker
of flames over the glowing coals and his father was smoking his
second pipe-full of tobacco, Elijah summoned the courage to approach him.

"May I speak with you, Father?"

His father didn't answer, but taking a long draw on his pipe,
he nodded.

After taking a deep breath to collect his thoughts, Elijah began. "Father, I have no desire to hurt you by going against your
wishes. I want you to understand that I'm almost a man and I do
have strong feelings for my country, as I know you have. To put it
quite simply, Father I . . . I wish to go to New York and enlist in
the Continental Army and fight for our country's independence."

Elijah stiffened himself and stood proudly. He realized with
some pleasure and pride, that he had just made a plea for his own
personal independence. His mother had a worried look on her
face. She had stopped her mending when Elijah first started to
speak, now with a half smile on her lips and fear in her eyes, she
looked at her husband. Both she and her proud son awaited his
answer, but each waited and prayed for a different reply.

Thomas Churchill got up from his well worn, over stuffed
chair and went to the fire. Tapping on the stone hearth, he watched

the remnants of burned tobacco fall from his pipe. The glow from the dying fire lighted the features of a stern man. With slow deliberation, he turned to answer his son. He wore the expression of a man who was resolute in his decision. He turned his back to the fire to face his son. The fire flared up and Elijah could no longer clearly see his father's face and perhaps that was of some help for both of them.

"Elijah, this is the last time I will speak to you on this matter. I do not expect, nor will I tolerate, any discussion," bellowed the powerfully built man.

"Yes, Father, I understand."

"I admire your desire to fight for this fine land of ours. I'm proud of the way you've come to me, as a man, or almost a man as you have said. But, you're just that, almost a man, you're too young to enlist. There are others who have enlisted and many more who will, but you'll not be numbered among them. I forbid you to go to New York. I forbid you to even try to enlist. That's my final word on this matter. Good night, Elijah."

"Good night, Father."

Elijah went over to where his mother was sitting. She had resumed her mending, but again stopped as her son approached. Elijah bent down and kissed her on the forehead. She saw his determined look and with a breathy voice she whispered softly, "Elijah, no!"

"Good night, Mother," said Elijah as he smiled at his mother and kissed her forehead once again. A warmth came over him and he was pleased. At least she understood him and what he was about to do. He also knew, intuitively, that she would not mention her fears to his father, but instead, tonight her pillow would be wet with her tears.

Much later that night, with his family asleep and the house graveyard-still, Elijah packed an extra shirt and a pair of trousers in a blanket roll, and left home. He walked the old mule some distance before mounting. After a long sad look back at his home of thirteen years, he headed toward the Tallmadge farm.

TWO

The June night was unusually cold and Elijah kept the blanket wrapped tightly around him. He was thankful for the heat from the mule which warmed him somewhat. Hidden in the trees near the Tallmadge farmhouse, he waited patiently for the lieutenant to leave. Several times he almost fell asleep, but a shudder or sound from the mule woke him from his lethargy and he continued his vigil with new determination.

Shortly before dawn, he heard Benjamin Tallmadge and his father make their farewells on the farmhouse porch. As Benjamin mounted his horse, Elijah moved the mule deeper into the thicket of trees so he could not be seen as the rider passed. After a few moments, as the sound of hoof beats was fading away, Elijah urged his old mule out onto the road and followed the horse and its rider.

*

Approaching the mid-morning hour by Elijah's estimates, he passed through the village of Smithtown. He followed Tallmadge at quite a distance, to be sure that he would not be seen. It appeared to the young boy that the lieutenant was in no hurry to report to his regiment. He had set a pace that even the old mule had no trouble maintaining. Elijah knew that by now his family was aware he had run away from home.

They would presume, correctly, that he had run away to join the army of the revolution to fight for freedom and independence. His chest filled with pride as he thought of all the gallant and heroic deeds he just knew he would perform. He tortured himself with thoughts of the sadness he had seen in his mother's eyes as with a barely audible voice she had whispered, "Elijah, no!" Thoughts of his father came to him and he spurred his mule on, even though he knew that his father would not be following.

He soon became hungry and wished that he had brought food instead of clothes in the blanket roll. Perhaps he could find a garden with some fruit or vegetables. He disliked the thought of stealing, but his hunger pains were quite real. His hunger forced memories of last night's stew with the fresh bread and potatoes. He allowed his mind to wander as his craving for food brought pleasant thoughts of delicious foods he wished were now set before him.

Abruptly he realized that the road ahead was clear for at least a quarter of a mile and Tallmadge was no where in sight. Had he stopped to rest? Was there a farmhouse ahead? Where did he go? This was the only road. He had to be up ahead. Elijah kicked the mule into a faster pace.

Estimating that he was somewhere between the villages of Huntington and Oyster Bay, he noticed that the trees were more dense in this area. He was concerned that he might come across Tallmadge resting under one of the trees which now crowded the dusty road. Should he proceed slowly so as not to be seen by Tallmadge or continue this faster pace until he once again saw him on the road ahead? He decided quickly and urged the mule into a gallop.

A shout! He heard the thundering sound of a horse at full gallop bearing down on him. Tallmadge came, seemingly out of nowhere, overwhelming Elijah. He had no control over the mule and then he realized that Tallmadge had taken hold of the mule's bridle and was pulling both horse and mule to a halt. Both animals grunted loudly as they were forced together. A choking cloud of dust settled around them and Elijah found himself looking into the angry face and piercing blue eyes of Lieutenant Benjamin Tallmadge.

"Why are you following me, boy?"

"I . . . I was . . . " stammered Elijah.

"You're the boy I met yesterday. Elijah? Yes, the name was Elijah. Now tell me. Why are you following me?"

"I was not following you." Elijah lied and spoke rapidly, his voice rising in pitch.

The lieutenant glared at him. It was obvious that his anger was mounting and that he had no time for foolishness.

"I'm sorry, sir, that was a lie," his voice became subdued. "I was following you. I want to go to New York and enlist in the army. We spoke of this yesterday and . . . "

"Go home! I do not want the responsibility of bringing one as young as you onto the battlefield. You think only of glory and valor. You see yourself leading a gallant charge of cavalry with your sword raised. In truth, war is an indescribable horror. Many will die and they'll die a terrible death. Others will be maimed, losing an arm or a leg and carrying the so-called glory of war for the rest of their lives. Go home!" Benjamin shouted at Elijah and threw the reins in his face. The frightened mule side stepped away as Benjamin's horse reared up. Benjamin glanced angrily at Elijah and then sped off at a gallop.

Elijah did not move. He once again watched horse and rider disappear in the distance. He knew that he could not follow. He also knew that he could not go home. Elijah hung his head, not knowing which way to turn. At that moment he became more positive and determined than ever. He resolved to go to New York and at least try to enlist in the army. He would certainly distinguish himself with gallant deeds of valor. He would help all he could because his country needed him! Blind to the dangers of war and deaf to the advise of his elders, Elijah turned the old mule westward once again, toward New York and the Continental army. What adventures were in store for him?

*

"Git otter the way, boy," screamed the impatient and intolerant mule team driver as sweat streamed down his face. His open shirt was already soaked through. Spots of mud, kicked back by the mules, gave both his skin and his clothes an odd pock marked appearance.

"Git, boy, git," shouted another driver as Elijah moved out of the way of the first. He had never seen so many people in one place at one time. The construction of the fortifications at Brooklyn Heights was well under way. Teams of mules and oxen strained as they dragged the heavy timber into position. While prodding them with sticks, their drivers screamed and cursed at the wretched animals. Occasionally, the sizzle of a whip ripped through the air. Elijah thought of his old mule that had been taken from him just short of his Brooklyn Heights destination. He had been set upon by three men on horseback who just grabbed the mule, shoved him off, and rode away. There was very little, if anything, that he could have done about it, but nevertheless, he was in Brooklyn Heights and he didn't feel very much like a hero.

Noise, commotion, and an odd combination of mud on the ground and dust in the air was everywhere. The smells of sweating men and animals were mixed with the all too familiar odor of manure, which made Elijah think of the barn on his father's farm. But noxious odors were not the only smells in the air this day and Elijah continued to follow his nose.

Through all of the stench of animals and men, he could still pick out the beautiful aroma of freshly baked biscuits. He had not eaten since he had left home early yesterday morning and his stomach was letting him know about it. Without too much trouble he managed to find the source of the tantalizing odor. As he rounded several rather large outcrops of rock, he came upon an array of large cooking pots hanging from tripods over fires.

Large sections of beef and whole pigs were roasting on spits occasionally turned by the men who Elijah surmised were the army cooks. There were many men and each was busy at some task. Several men were stirring large pots, kneading dough, cutting vegetables, while others were building racks and tables and the like. They all had an urgency about them.

Elijah spied the biscuits and walked over to a batch of fifty or so. His mouth began to water as he reached for one and then stopped. No one appeared to be paying attention to him, but as hungry as he was, he still could not bring himself to steal. He called out to the cooks and the other men, but he was ignored. Then he saw his salvation. Out of the corner of his eye, he spied one biscuit that had fallen on the ground. Surely, no one would mind if he took a soiled biscuit. He stooped to reach for it and he felt a strong hand grasp the back of his shirt and lift him off the ground into the air and then back on his feet.

"Are you hungry, boy?" asked a large burly, bald headed man.

Elijah looked up at him. He was at least six foot four inches tall and Elijah wouldn't even guess at his weight. He was as round as he was tall and presented a frightening image to the young boy. Then the man smiled at him and Elijah could tell that he was looking at a gentle giant.

"Yes, sir, I am. May I have that dirty biscuit? No one would want it," said Elijah as he pointed to the food on the ground.

"Don't call me sir. I'm not one of those damn 'holier than thou' officers. I'm a Sergeant. Sergeant Kowalski, chief cook of this man's army. Here, boy, if you're hungry have a fresh biscuit," said the cook as he gave Elijah a steaming hot one. "You'll find that it's better than any your mother ever made," bragged Kowalski as he watched the young boy gulp down the hot biscuit, his eyes pleading for more.

"What're you doing here? Don't you have a home?" he asked as he handed Elijah another biscuit. Elijah thought about the question and wondered if he still had a place that he could call home and if he would ever return.

"I intend to enlist and —" Elijah stopped as the cook leaned backward and roared with laughter.

"He intends to enlist! Did you hear that?" boomed the chief cook to all the others. The men stopped their work for a moment and looked at Elijah with amusement.

"But, I do, really, I do want to enlist," stammered Elijah somewhat embarrassed over the laughter that followed as he repeated his statement.

"Forget it, boy. You're too young. But if you want to hang around here and be part of the action, I have work that'll keep you busy. I could use a hand and I'll feed you as well. Well, what do you say? Speak up, boy."

"That would be just fine. I'll stay with you and help out, that is . . . until I can enlist."

Again the laughter, but Elijah didn't mind. Kowalski handed him another biscuit, and at least he was, as the chief cook had said, "part of the action".

*

The next few weeks were hectic for General Washington's fledgling army as the fortifications were near completion. Elijah had been kept very busy and was quickly learning that cooking for large groups of hungry men was no easy task. More and more soldiers joined the ranks of those already at the Brooklyn fortifications and Elijah had heard that equal numbers were ready just across the East River, in the city of New York. Elijah was amazed at the difference in style and color of the uniforms among the American troops. There was no continuity. Although arms and ammunition were the main concern of the leaders, most of them did provide uniforms. Each colony, and sometimes each regiment within the colony, was different. When you added the militia from each town, a rainbow of colors could best describe the American army. Most of the soldiers wore white or buff breeches. The jackets were basically blue with white facings, but some were brown or buff or even green. The Marylanders had green shirts and leggings to match as did the Green Mountain Boys from New Connecticut or Vermont, as they preferred to call their area of the country. The rifleman from New Jersey wore short red coats and striped trousers. The Pennsylnanians were literally in all hues of the rainbow. The Virginians were in white frocks with ruffles at the neck, elbows and wrists.

Hats ranged from plumed helmets to three-cornered hats and stocking caps of all colors. Some soldiers, much to Elijah's surprise, wore buckskin. Coming from the middle of Long Island, he had only seen Indians wearing animal skins. But, they were all soldiers, all American, all ready to fight to drive the English out of their country.

Spirits were high among all the soldiers. Elijah heard their comments on the chow line every evening.

"Those Redcoats don't have a chance."

"Can't wait 'til the shootin' starts."

"Where are they? They hidin' from us?"

"We're going to have to go lookin' for them." Each comment was met with laughter as jokes were passed around the encampment. Even the officers were amused, but they tried not to show it to those in their command. They maintained an aloofness from their men so that discipline could be sustained during battle.

Elijah wanted to be a soldier, but he had found out that the advise given to him from his father, Tallmadge, Kowalski, and others, was correct. He was just too young to be a soldier. He consoled himself that at least he was with the army.

In the next few weeks he heard that more and more English ships were reported to have anchored in New York harbor. One night a Maryland rifleman stood up from his evening meal and told a hushed crowd of soldiers that he had seen the fleet. He said that the masts, yardarms, and other riggings made the fleet resemble a vast forest of trimmed pine trees. He remarked that it looked as if all of London was afloat. After that night, the men didn't joke as readily as before. The great majority of them had never been in battle and the knowledge of being outnumbered, did not appeal to them. As more time passed, more ships came from England and many additional ships came from nearby Canada. By August, reports were that some 300 ships were anchored in the harbor.

The rumors filtered through the troops that the British wanted to destroy Washington's army quickly and thus stop the revolution. That was exactly what the British had in mind. The American officers said that it was only rumors, but in truth the British had more than 32,000 seasoned fighting men, greater than three times the size of the untried American forces. There were also reports of mercenary Hessian troops, numbering over 9,000 men. Stories of the lack of mercy of these hired soldiers were frightening. The American officers were doing their best, but failed to keep spirits high. The rumors, fed by the men's fear of the unknown, were now growing in disproportion to the truth.

One night a group of tired and hungry infantry men approached Elijah as he was cleaning pots and pans from the evening meal. All the men had become fond of him, but there were few that he could call friends.

"Elijah, could you get us something to eat? We couldn't get here for supper. A weak section of the west wall had to be redone and well . . . "

"I'll get you plenty to eat. How many are you?"

"Let's see now, we're five, no . . . better figure on six. Tallmadge will be coming along as well."

Elijah stiffened at the sound of the name. He had wondered when he would run into Lieutenant Benjamin Tallmadge. He wanted to run, but then realized that the Lieutenant could do him no harm nor would he want to. The soldiers collapsed on the ground in exhaustion. They rubbed their eyes and some fell asleep on the ground where they lay.

Elijah wondered what Lieutenant Tallmadge would say and do when he saw that he had not gone home as he had been told. He readied the food for the men and listened for the sound of an approaching horse which would herald the arrival of the dragoon officer.

The exhausted men sat in silence and soon another infantry man came to the cooking area.

"Over here, Will, over here," they called to him.

He smiled and waved when he saw them. He walked over to them and it was obvious that he, too, had been hard at work on the west wall. He was hungry and exhausted. He threw down his equipment and flopped on the ground.

"The boy, Elijah, he's getting us something to eat."

"Great, I'm starved," said the newcomer.

"Will there be seven now?" asked Elijah.

"No, only six, this is the man I spoke of. This is William Tallmadge."

So it's not the Lieutenant who was coming for late dinner, but his brother William, thought Elijah. Although he felt that he had nothing to hide or fear from the lieutenant, Elijah was still relieved to know there would be no unwanted confrontation. He had never met Benjamin's brother, but he knew of him and that he was the elder brother by about three or four years.

Elijah made a point of serving William Tallmadge last so that he could talk to him.

"I'm Elijah Churchill. My father has a farm near your father's farm in Brookhaven."

Tallmadge continued to eat and only stared at Elijah.

"You're from that same Tallmadge family, are you not?"

"Yes, boy, yes! But, I'm tired and hungry and I don't feel much like conversation!" growled William.

Elijah looked dejected and started to walk away. What is it with this Tallmadge family, thought Elijah. Do I bring out the worst in them? They never have a kind word for me.

Elijah was surprised when William called out to him. "Wait, don't leave, sit down, boy. I'm sorry I snapped at you, but I am tired. Let me eat and rest a while, and then we'll talk about our home town. His smile was warm and friendly. Elijah dutifully sat down next to William and waited for him to finish his supper.

Most of the men had fallen asleep. Elijah managed to get a tankard of wine from the chief cook's personal supplies and gave it to Will. They talked for a long time about Brookhaven and Setauket and the people that they both knew. Elijah deliberately didn't mention Benjamin Tallmadge, but eventually he was brought into the conversation.

"My brother Benjamin is also here. He's my younger brother, by four years, and I'm very proud of him. He's an officer."

"Yes, I know," said Elijah hesitantly. "I met the Lieutenant when he visited your father in Brookhaven," said Elijah.

"Lieutenant? That was two months ago. He's now Major Tallmadge, mind you that, and he's an aide to General Washington. That's why I'm so proud of that brother of mine!"

"Then you've seen him?"

"Yes. After he found out what regiment I served in, he had me summoned to his headquarters. His headquarters, do you hear that! I wasn't told the name of the officer who wanted to see me, so I was wondering what trouble I'd gotten myself into. When I saw that the major who wanted me was my brother, we both started jumping around and yelling. We were so loud that all the guards came in with weapons ready. Can you imagine? We both laughed at them. Yes, Elijah, I've seen my brother."

*

In the next week Elijah and William spoke often and despite the difference in age, became close friends. Will was like an older brother to Elijah. They talked about what a battle might be like as William had not seen any fighting. They wondered what it might feel like to be shot. William knew that his new friend wanted to be a soldier so he taught him the little that he knew about guns, the army, and a little about warfare that he had been told by officers and the few others who had been in battle.

Elijah was familiar with guns. He had hunted rabbit, squirrel, and wild turkey ever since he was ten years old. He was considered a good shot and had always won the turkey shooting contest at the church gatherings every fall. It was seldom that a fox lived through a raid on their chicken coop. The barn door on his father's farm always sported a fox skin as Elijah's latest trophy.

As time passed, everyone knew that the English would not sit still very much longer. Tension grew among the men as they read-

ied themselves for the unknown. Elijah was always full of questions and he kept asking William if he had any new information.
"Do you think the attack will come today?"

"It will come soon enough. I don't know when, but when it
happens there'll be no mistaking it. You'll know."

"Will, when the fighting starts, I'll come to you, wherever you
are."

"You'll do no such thing! No, Elijah, you stay where it's safe."

"But, I want to help."

William Tallmadge just smiled and lightly cuffed his young
friend on the chin.

In the last week of August, several British ships left their New
York anchorage and sailed to the south of Brooklyn and anchored
off-shore at Gravesend. The patriots didn't know it, but the invasion of Long Island had begun.

THREE

"Where will you be when the fighting starts?" asked Elijah, "I bet you'll be on the west wall, where everyone says the main attack will come."

"No chance of that. They're sticking me and a couple of thousand men about two miles south of here on a high ridge called the Heights of Guam or something like that," said William.

"Why there?"

"I overheard the officers talking. We're either a reserve unit or they are worried about an attack on the flank. What fools they are. The British will hit the west wall of this place with everything they have. Our officers are weakening us by this partial move to the south. General Putnam is a good man, but he doesn't know what he is doing. I heard two officers arguing about the lay of the land. They said that Putnam doesn't know how or where to place the men. To top it all, Putnam has placed General Sullivan in charge of the southern defenses. Talk about the blind leading the blind, Sullivan knows less than Putnam. The men are . . . "

"Your regiment has a general to lead you? How exciting!" said Elijah.

"That's one thing this army has plenty of, . . . generals, but we still don't know where the enemy is going to strike or with how many men."

"When will you be going to these new southern fortifications?'

"I'll be leaving early this afternoon, but my friend, there really isn't any fortification. I've been told that we'll just dig in on the ridge."

*

Early that afternoon, Will Tallmadge's regiment was gathering outside the southern gate for their march to the Heights of Guam. They were called into order and they formed their ranks, four abreast. William positioned himself on an outside line so he could talk to Elijah. As they started off, Elijah walked with him and they continued talking.

"Be careful, Will."

"Be careful of what? There are no English where we're going. You be careful here, and when the fighting starts, stay out of it. Say, are you going to walk all the way with me? Stay here, Elijah, my friend, I'll see you later."

"Much sooner than you think. Late tonight, or early tomorrow morning, Sergeant Kowalski, the chief cook, will be taking supplies to the 'Sullivan Command'. I begged him so much, that he's letting me go with him. So, I will see you."

Elijah stopped walking and waved to his friend who turned and winked at him. The 'Sullivan Command' marched off and although everyone knew that there would be no fighting, still Elijah wished that he too, was in uniform and marching with them.

*

The wagon was large and it took most of the night for Elijah and the sergeant to load it and hitch up the mule team. It was about two o'clock in the morning when they finally climbed aboard and called to the mules. The six mules strained to get the wagon started. They had traveled only a very short distance and then . . . gunfire! A clamor and commotion arose at the west wall. The British were attacking exactly where Will said they would. Elijah heard rapid cannon fire. Flashes of light from the explosions, briefly filled the sky. The Americans were returning the fire. The battle for Brooklyn was underway.

The heavy wagon lumbered along and Elijah looked at Sergeant Kowalski in disbelief.

"Aren't we going back?"

"We all have jobs to do in this man's army. Our job is to deliver these supplies."

Elijah sputtered and stammered a moment then realized that he knew better than to try to change the sergeant's mind. He looked over his shoulder back toward the fort as it now could only be seen when illuminated by cannon fire. He thought of his desire, his dream, to be gallant and heroic, but he would not be in this battle. When would he get a chance to fight for his country? It should be now, he thought, it should be now. It will be now! Elijah made a move to the side of the wagon and braced himself to jump off. He felt the grip of Kowalski's large hand upon his shoulder.

"Stay here, boy. I'd like to be with them much more than you, but as I've said, we all have our jobs to do."

Kowalski removed his hand from Elijah's shoulder and looked at him. He tilted his head and questioned with his eyes. Elijah nodded yes, but was none too happy that he had resigned himself to doing nothing. Kowalski looked back toward the sounds of battle. At that moment Elijah realized that Kowalski wanted to be an infantryman, not a cook! What twist of fate had kept him from his desires? The sergeant clicked his tongue at the mules and they now moved along at a faster pace.

They had traveled more than half the distance to their destination and neither of them had spoken. Each was deep in his own thoughts as the sound of the fighting at Brooklyn Heights faded into an all too real memory that would not leave them. On occasion, the flash of cannon fire was seen, but only if they happened to be looking toward the north. When the sounds and sights of battle passed completely, the lack of conversation became more and more apparent, but the two rode on in an ever more embarrassing silence. The only sounds were the creaking of the wagon and the functional sound of the leather harness straining with the mules. It was a hot foggy night and occasionally a snort or grunt from a mule would punctuate the wagon sounds. It appeared to both of them that at any moment either might speak and break the stillness, but they continued in silence.

With only about a quarter of a mile to go, they started to hear gunfire once again. Kowalski stopped the mules. They both looked northward and strained their ears in the silence to hear. There it was again! Unmistakable sounds of muskets, but it was coming from ahead of them. Could the 'Sullivan Command' be under attack?

Sergeant Kowalski reached for his whip. It sang as it sliced through the thick early morning air and spurred the mules on-ward. They quickly closed the distance between themselves and the increasing sounds of battle. There was a rise in the road ahead of them and the mules climbed the hill. Flashes of gunfire could be seen just over the crest. Kowalski stopped the mules and leaped off the wagon with Elijah right on his heels. They ran to the sound of battle. Nearing the edge, they crept low on the ground through the underbrush. At the edge, they parted the thick growth of the remaining tall weeds and peered through them. A gasp escaped the lips of Elijah. The battle was at its height. Redcoats were everywhere. The smell of gunpowder and the shouts and screams of men filled the air. Clouds of dust and smoke rolled over the battle scene, making it difficult to see in the half light of early morning. Here and there, in the flashes of light, the colors of the uniforms could be seen. The predominant color was red. The British flag was everywhere, but where was the gallant liberty flag?

"Where are our men?" asked Elijah.

"There," said Kowalski, as he looked around and then pointed toward an entrenchment of infantrymen at the edge of the cliffs. "There they are, and they are pinned down by a force ten times their size. This is the main attack! The attack on the west wall was only a rouse."

"What can we do to help them?" said Elijah as thoughts of his friend, Will, came to him.

"They're surrounded with no means of escape. If they stay there, they haven't got a chance and I can't see any means of escape. We got to do something," said the sergeant.

"Let's go down there and do what we can."

"Don't be foolish, boy. We have no weapons and even if we did, we would just be two more added to the slaughter."

"We've got to do something!" said Elijah. He spoke bravely, but was frightened for himself and at the same time worried about his friend. The expression on the sergeant's face told Elijah that an idea, a plan, was forming in his mind. Kowalski's face had an encouraging smile as he turned to Elijah. "We're going to cut a path through those Redcoats so our men can escape."

"We?"

"We, and the mules and . . . and that big wagon!" He spoke with a gleam in his eye that foretold of the possibility of success. They crawled backwards for a short distance and then ran to the wagon, startling the mules. Sergeant Kowalski backed the mules and wagon away from the crest of the hill. "The mules will have to get a running start to be able to come over the top of the hill with power and speed," explained Kowalski. Before starting the mules, Kowalski searched the wagon for two large barrels of gun powder. He broke both of them open, spilling the black powder all over the wagon and the supplies.

Somehow, I'll ignite them, Kowalski thought. "You stay here," he admonished Elijah.

"Not on your life! I'm going with you," announced a surprised and frightened Elijah.

"Then climb aboard, boy. We got a job to do!"

Elijah climbed up on the wagon along side the chief cook, now turned army strategist. The long whip snapped and cracked over the nervous heads of the six mules as they pulled and strained. Under the encouragement of the whip they moved the wagon along faster and faster. The mule team and the huge wagon driven by the two hopeful rescuers, mounted the crest of the hill and plummeted down the other side ripping through the midst of the startled Redcoats. A frightened Elijah added his screams to Kowalski's roar as the whip ripped at the crazed animals now wild with fear.

"Yeeeaaaahhhh, yeeeeeaaaaaahhhh," they screamed. Barrels and large heavy packages of foodstuffs, peppered with gunpowder, bounced off the wagon on its suicide mission. The British were so taken by surprise that some dropped their weapons and fled from the path of the wagon and its crazed team of mules. Many British fell and were crushed by the hooves of the mules or under the heavy wagon wheels. Others were sent crashing into their fellows by the barrels that rolled down upon them. Gunpowder cascaded from the open sides of the wagon. Kowalski hoped that the powder still in the barrels and in the wagon would not ignite until he touched a match to the black explosive.

The remnants of the 'Sullivan Command' saw the wagon as it cut a swath through the Redcoats as clean as a scythe cuts through fresh grass. The remaining officers saw their means of escape and rallied their men to take it. The Americans shouted and charged up the hill before the Redcoats could recover from the startling, devastating effect of the mules, the wagon, and its cargo. Flash fires, caused by the loose gunpowder somehow igniting on the ground, added to the confusion.

The wagon plunged downward and came to a sudden abrupt halt as the front wheels dropped into the first trench. The two occupants were pitched out of the wagon onto the ground as the wagon crashed into the screaming mules. Elijah saw the sergeant pick up a rifle and take gunpowder and shot from a dead soldier. He wanted to do the same and fight as well, but first he had to find his friend, Will.

Elijah ran through the trenches. Musket shot whistled around him and he was surprised that he was no longer frightened. A British soldier stood up and took aim at Elijah. To Elijah amazement, the soldier dropped his weapon and grasped his throat as a musket ball ripped into him. The soldier fell backwards into the trench and stared at the ever brightening sky with sightless eyes.

It seemed to Elijah that he would never find Will. He hoped that he had not been killed, but was now fearful that he would find his friend lying dead in some trench. All around him, and everywhere he looked, were the dead and the dying. Elijah turned over the bodies of some who were the same size and wore the same uniform as his friend. He was nearing the end of the entrench-ments and near the end of hope, when he heard his name being called.

"Elijah, over here, Elijah!"

Elijah turned to see his friend, Will, propped up along the side of the trench. He was grasping his shoulder and was obviously in severe pain. Elijah could see blood oozing from between Will's fingers.

"You're hurt, Will. We have to get you out of here."

"You get yourself out of here, and now! What are you doing here?" gasped William as shuddered with pain. "We wondered what it would feel like to be shot. Well, it's not nice."

William laughed and his attempt at smiling quickly turned into a grimace. He closed his eyes as a sharp flow of pain ebbed through his body.

"Will, what happened? Why was the main attack here?"

"I told you . . . about the blind leading the . . . the blind. Nobody . . . nobody knows . . . nothing!"

Will was pale from loss of blood and sweating profusely. He shivered as a chill moved through his body.

Elijah moved to help Will as a large explosion rocked the battle-field and threw him to the ground. Elijah felt the force of the blast through the ground around him and knew that the fires, or Kowalski, had reached the barrels of gunpowder.

"How bad is that wound? Is that . . . "

"Look out!" shouted Will as he pushed Elijah out the line of fire and took a musket shot in his thigh. His body shuddered with pain. The Redcoat who had fired the shot was reloading his mus-ket as quickly as possible. Elijah knew that the next shot would soon tear into him. He spied Will's rifle by his side and picked it up.

"It's loaded," yelled Will.

With an ease that Elijah felt uncomfortable with, he sent a musket ball into the forehead of the Redcoat. Another Redcoat appeared. His rifle was loaded and Elijah could only watch as he raised it and took aim directly at Elijah's head. A shot rang out and Elijah's would be killer fell dead on the ground.

"Git, outa here, boy" said Sergeant Kowalski as he was reloading his musket. "I'll cover you. Go, now. Run for it!"

"I can shoot, too," said Elijah as he took Will's shot bag and gunpowder horn to reload. More Redcoats appeared, each ready to fire their rifles. Sergeant Kowalski stepped in front of Elijah, his body stopping most of the musket balls. The big man staggered and fell backward on top of Elijah. Elijah felt a sharp pain in his head. He was loosing consciousness and he fought to stay alert. Elijah felt like a drowning man struggling for just one more breath. He felt himself slipping into darkness. The pain increased just before everything went black.

*

Elijah awoke with a pounding pain in his head and found it not only difficult to breath, but also to move. He pushed and shoved and squirmed his way out from under Sergeant Kowalski's dead body. He looked upon the man who had saved his life. The big man lay on his back with his arms spread, his eyes and mouth wide open. Elijah wanted to do something for the man, but it had been too late for him for many hours. Then Elijah thought of Will. He turned and looked at the spot where he had last seen his friend. Will was gone. He could not have left under his own power. It was obvious that William Tallmadge had been taken by the enemy.

Elijah looked about him. The sun was setting. He had been unconscious most of the daylight hours. Suddenly he felt sick and nauseous. He tried to remember what had happened. The sergeant had taken all of the musket shots and then had fallen hard on top of him. He remembered hitting his head on something rock-hard on the side of the trench and then passing out. He rubbed his head where it still ached. An uncomfortable feeling of sticky dampness was virtually all over his body. It was then he noticed that his clothing was soaked through. He was covered with Sergeant Kowalski's blood. He quickly stood up, as if to get away from the sickly mess, and a wave of nausea came over him. He braced himself against the side of the trench, but still felt as if he was falling. At first the nausea passed, but as he looked around at the dead bodies and the pools of blood, he began to wretch and then vomit. When the sickness passed, he took off his blood soaked clothing as quickly as he could.

Elijah walked about the entrenchments. The Redcoats had left. In the twilight glow of the early evening, the battlefield was still and silent. Large black crows walked around and over the bodies. Their attitude of aloofness in the presence of so much death, annoyed Elijah and he shouted until they flew away. The stench of gunpowder and blood lingered in the air. He gave up counting the bodies of the dead as he wandered through the battlefield. Small fires were still flickering, and other fire-burned areas were smoldering. He found two barrels of water untouched by the battle. He opened the top of one and washed his face and hands. He opened the other barrel and drank his fill of water not bloodied by his hands or face. He tore a piece of discarded battalion flag and after dipping it into the first barrel, began to scrub off the horrors of war. He scrubbed until his skin was raw, dipping the cloth many, many times into the clear water. Faster and faster he rubbed until he heard the sound of someone crying. He stopped suddenly and raised his head to listen. He realized then that it was he who had been crying.

Elijah drank again and looked about for something to wear. He refused to even think of wearing his own clothes. He looked for a soldier, about his size, whose uniform he felt would fit him. Unfortunately, he had many to choose from. He disdained to wear a British uniform, so he only looked among the American dead. He found a soldier about his size whose uniform was relatively clean. He removed the uniform from the body and put it on. It had been his intention to only find suitable clothing, but when he saw the uniform jacket lying on the ground, he put it on, slowly,

deliberately, and with great reverence. He noticed a hole created
by a musket shot, on the left side over the heart. The blood stain
had started to turn purple. Elijah knew that this was the shot that
had killed the previous owner of the jacket. He looked upon it as
an emblem of honor. Elijah thought for a moment and then quickly
took the pouches of powder and shot and slung them over his
shoulder. He lifted the boy's rifle from the ground and ran his
hands over the smooth stock and barrel. The soldier's hat lay at his
feet. He picked it up and placed it upon his head. The picture was
now complete. He looked at the dead soldier who lay on the ground.
He didn't appear to be much older than Elijah. This could have
been me, he thought, but now he's dead and I wear his uniform.
Elijah had been too young to enlist, but in his heart he had done
just that. He was now an American soldier.

Before setting out on the long walk to the Brooklyn Height
encampment, he went to Sergeant Kowalski's body. He crossed
the arms over the dead man's chest, placed blanket roll under the
head and gently closed the chief cook's eyes. He found another
blanket roll, opened it and placed it over the body. Saying a short
prayer, he stood up and saluted the memory of a friend.

*

When Elijah Churchill finally made his way back to Brooklyn
Heights that night, he found the army in disarray. The loss of so
many men was extremely difficult for the untried troops to com-
prehend and fathom. General Washington had been at the fortifications all day, and when news came of the massive defeat coupled
with the capture of Generals Stirling and Sullivan, he sent to New
York for reinforcements. The fledgling army waited for the attack
they knew would finish them and their righteous cause. Washington and his officers were seen virtually everywhere throughout the
fortification, encouraging the men and rallying them to the flag of
liberty and freedom.

Elijah was also all over the fortification, but unlike the general and the officers, he was only after one man. He was looking for Major Benjamin Tallmadge. Every soldier and officer he approached told him that the major was somewhere in the stronghold, probably with General Washington. That, he already knew and he continued his search. Later in the night Elijah came upon a small group of officers, standing near a rather large fire. They were listening intently to one man. Elijah knew, even from a distance, that the man was General Washington.

Staying well outside the outer circle of the glow of the fire, Elijah circled the officers. He studied the face of each man until he came upon the face of Benjamin Tallmadge. His heart leaped a beat when he noticed that he bore a striking resemblance to his friend, Will. The resemblance had somehow escaped him, when looking at Will. At least an hour had passed before the general dismissed most of the officers. Only Major Tallmadge and another officer, a captain, remained with the general. The three began to walk away and Elijah followed, hoping to speak to Tallmadge when he was alone. They must have heard him following, for the trio stopped and turned around. Elijah was frightened and awed at being in the presence of General Washington. He felt that he didn't belong and wanted to run, but he stood his ground as General Washington spoke to him in a kindly manner. "Yes, soldier, what is it you want?"

"Forgive me, sir, I don't wish to intrude, but may I have a word with the Major?" Seeing the quizzical look on the faces of the officers, he quickly added, "I have news about his brother."

Major Tallmadge looked at his general.

"Go, Benjamin, find out about your brother. Report to me later," said the general as he turned and walked away with the other officer. Benjamin saluted the departing general and ran to Elijah's side. Elijah backed away and Benjamin followed.

"Stand still, soldier. What news have you about my brother?" said Tallmadge as he again tried to approach Elijah. Elijah walked over to the fire and began to warm his hands from the sudden chill in the night.

"Speak up, soldier, what word have you for me?" repeated Benjamin, who was becoming quite angry. He reached for Elijah and turned him around. Elijah looked at the major and as the firelight flickered across his face, Benjamin Tallmadge recognized him.

"Well, Elijah Churchill, and in uniform. How did you get that uniform?" thundered Tallmadge in a rage. Elijah pulled out of his grasp. "I . . . I earned it today. I was with your brother, William, when the Redcoats ran over our position. We must've lost a thousand —"

"We lost fifteen hundred men, but please, tell me of Will," said Benjamin, his anger calming quickly.

"He was wounded, twice, and he saved my life. I was knocked unconscious and when I awoke . . . he was gone."

"Gone? What do you mean, gone? Is . . . is my brother dead?" asked Benjamin softly.

"The British must have taken him. He had to be captured. If he were dead, the Redcoats would have left him there."

The major looked deeply pensive for a moment, then he looked at the young boy standing before him. He reached out and fingered the dried blood-stained hole in the uniform which was directly over the heart.

"How did you come to be in the trenches with my brother?"

"We were . . . we are friends."

"That really doesn't explain your being there. How did you manage to live through this musket shot?"

Elijah didn't answer him, nor could he look at the major. He lowered his head and stared at his feet.

"Elijah, it would be best if you . . . "

Elijah irrupted from his silence, his jaw set with determination. "No. I'll not go home, sir, I may not have entered it properly and according to all the rules, but I'm in the army now and I'll stay until the war is over or until I'm dead. No, sir, I'll not go home!"

"You don't realize it, boy, but we may all be dead by tomorrow. No, Elijah, I'll not send you home. God knows what you've gone through since I last saw you. May God bless this country and those like you who are willing to die for it."

"Sir, you had asked about . . . about this uniform. I want you to know that I'll never dishonor it and —"

"The 'and' doesn't matter now, Elijah. How you got that uniform and how someone wearing that particular uniform was there in that regiment and in that . . . that massacre, doesn't matter now. Perhaps our lives are destined to be interwoven."

"How so, sir?"

"That uniform that you somehow inherited, was worn by a private in the Connecticut Second Regiment of Light Dragoons. Through a quirk of fate, you, Private Elijah Churchill, are in my regiment and under my command!"

FOUR

The morning came slowly. No color appeared in the eastern sky, just a gradual change from black to lighter shades of dull gray. The Americans had waited throughout the night for the inevitable British attack, but it never came. Instead, rain became their foe. It was certain that the Redcoats would charge their position and they were now having difficulty keeping their firearms and powder dry. Washington had placed additional lookouts on the walls and sent small scouting parties toward the enemy lines. Where were the English? What were they planning? When will they strike? These unanswered questions preyed on the minds of the men.

These same questions bothered General Washington and his staff as well. The officers tried to keep the soldier's spirits high as they circulated throughout the remaining regiments. The exhausted men grumbled about the waiting, the lack of dry powder and the incessant rain which pelted them without pity.

After a few hours the officers were looking at each other in dismay. How long would this go on? A prevailing silence began as the men stopped their complaining. All that was heard was the sound of intense rain. The deluge fell steadily without a stop, blanketing the entire encampment with a sound which amplified the gloom and despair of the men.

The lack of action coupled with the possibility of attack at any moment caused a weird mixture of anxiety and depression. The men were tired and many had lost friends in the 'Sullivan Command', but the uncertainty of when the Redcoats would attack and the strong possibility of joining those fallen comrades kept them awake. Nevertheless, word came down that they should try

to sleep if they could. Each officer divided his command so that at
least half would be ready at a moments notice.

The officers also rested in shifts although most of them preferred to set an example for their men by staying awake. Most of
Major Tallmadge's regiment was in New York and he was here
only as an aide to General Washington. He had no troops to command and yet he stayed with the enlisted men trying to heighten
their spirits while spreading hope and courage.

The morning gave way to the afternoon and the rain continued unabated. The wads of cloth, and in some cases, the jackets of
the men which were used to protect the powder became soaked
with rain water. There was great concern as to whether their muskets and cannon would fire at all. There was no mess call as fires
would be impossible in the down pour from the unrelenting skies.
The men shared what little food they had with each other. The
minutes dragged on into hours and slowly the day eroded away.

Major Tallmadge finally gave in to exhaustion and went to the
officers tent. He laid down with thoughts of only resting but soon
succumbed to sleep. By nightfall the rain had stopped but still no
attack by the British. A heavy fog slowly crept into the encampment. It was impossible for the lookouts and sentries to see more
than a few feet ahead of them and they began to rely on the possibility that they might hear the approach of the enemy.

Word came down to the officers that Washington was calling a
staff meeting. Benjamin Tallmadge awoke from a deep sleep annoyed that he had allowed himself to doze at such a crucial time.
Putting on his coat and buckling on his sword, as he was leaving the
tent he stumbled and almost fell over Elijah sitting just outside.

"What the devil?" said Tallmadge as he regained his balance.

"It's only me, sir. Private Churchill."

"What're you doing here?"

"I didn't know what to do or where to go, sir. I don't know
where our, er, your regiment is, sir."

"The regiment is in New York," said the Major and with a
smile added. "I guess everybody has to be somewhere. You come

with me. I want you where I can keep an eye on you. I'll keep you out of trouble."

"What do I do, sir?"

"Just stay with me. How long ago did the rain stop and when did this confounded fog start?"

"Both about two hours ago, sir. But the fog has been getting steadily thicker and thicker."

The young major and the boy private moved as quickly as the fog would allow to the tent that had been set up for General Washington. Other officers bumped into them as they hurried to the meeting. When they arrived at Washington's tent, Elijah started to enter with Major Tallmadge. Again with a smile Tallmadge said, "I know I said that you should come with me, but I think it best that you wait outside."

"Yes, sir," said Elijah, but he waited until the major had entered the tent then he slipped just inside the flap and stood at attention in the shadows.

The general's tent was well lighted and he stood by a table in the center and drew his officers around him. On the table was a map of the fortifications, Brooklyn, New York, and the various waterways about them. General Washington waited for the last of his officers to arrive, and then, tapping with a riding croup against the maps, he began to speak. The men were silent. The impassive gaze of the general's blue eyes would silence any man.

"Gentleman, you all know that our situation is a precarious one. We've been weakened by our defeat in battle two days ago. This heavy rain has dampened our spirits as well as our gun-powder. I don't know why the British have not attacked. We have no information as to the exact strength of the enemy or when and where they will strike. But, this fog may be a blessing to us. I have stopped reinforcements from coming over from New York and have formulated an evacuation plan for these fortifications."

A mumble of dissent arose from the officers, but General Washington quickly quieted them by raising his hands. The officers were again silent as they looked to their leader.

"I appreciate the bravery of my officers, but our goal is to win this war for independence, not to die gallantly here in Brooklyn Heights. We will not sit and wait for death. We will evacuate and join our troops in New York. We will live to fight at another time in another field of glory. Obviously the British think they can destroy us any time they want, otherwise they would have initiated an offensive. But I must have information, some intelligence as to the enemy's strength and whereabouts, where they are moving, when, and how quickly. Lt. Colonel Thomas Knowlton, I put you to task to find one man, a volunteer, to gain such information for us. Have him report to me at our New York headquarters."

"Excuse me, sir," said Major Tallmadge. "I'd like to be that man. I volunteer."

"Thank you, Major, but I need you with me. Knowlton will find us a volunteer. Now, as to the evacuation. We must take advantage of this fog and move our men, regiment by regiment to the East River. We have formidable obstacles. The British appear to have three times the men we have. They are well disciplined and have a fleet capable of stopping any navigation. Despite all this, we must and will succeed. Colonel Glover's regiment of Massachusetts fishermen will handle the boats necessary for the crossing. The walls of this fortification will be manned until the last possible moment. Each regiment will retire from the lines of the front in such a manner that no chasm will be left that the British might notice. The first regiment will move out in two hours. May God be with us."

The evacuation proceeded without flaw. The regiments, approximately nine thousand men, were moved quietly to the boats at the East River and were ferried across to safety. The fog was now their ally. So smoothly did the withdrawal go that the Redcoats never knew they were gone. General Washington had saved the day for the young country.

Glover's Marbleheaders had gathered together a motley flotilla of whaleboats, barges, rowboats, scows, and canoes. Hundreds of wounded had been carried on litters, their anguish and pain increased with every movement. The bandages were red with blood from the reopening of the wounds.

As the last ferry was loading men, baggage, weapons, horses, and mules, a smaller vessel came to the wharf to take the last to leave. General Washington hurried his remaining officers on board. Major Tallmadge, waiting with Elijah, his new young orderly, requested a moment from his leader.

"General, sir, I request permission to stay behind."

"Speak up, Benjamin, and quickly, we have little time."

"As you know, my brother was wounded and captured. I request permission to try to find him and secure his escape."

Elijah stepped forward and started to speak. "I also would like . . ."

He was quickly waved into silence by Major Tallmadge. The general smiled at Elijah and then moved to his officer's side. Placing his hand on Benjamin's shoulder he spoke to him in a fatherly manner.

"Benjamin, Benjamin. We have just evacuated over nine thousand men because we knew that we were outnumbered by the enemy and now you want to attack them alone." General Washington stole a glance at Elijah who looked as if he were about to speak.

"Benjamin, I cannot allow this. Too many fine men have been lost. I need you with me. We have a war to win. I also have concern for those who were captured and if at all possible they will be saved. As to your brother, the English are civilized people, they will tend to his wounds and feed him. Your brother would not want you to throw your life away. Now, come, . . . on to New York."

Washington turned briskly and walked to the boat. Major Tallmadge followed, then almost as if he had read Elijah's mind he turned and grabbed the boy by the wrist just as Elijah started to run.

"Where do you think you're going." said Tallmadge his voice volume curtailed.

"But, Will is, . . . is somewhere back there."

"Somewhere? Somewhere? The general is right. I can't help William and neither can you," said Benjamin trying to keep his voice down. "Try to see and remember the bigger picture. We are all expendable, but this nation must survive. We do what we can, when we can. Do you understand that, Private Churchill?"

Benjamin Tallmadge looked at the young boy standing before him whose eyes were on the verge of tears. Throwing his arm over the boy's shoulder, he spoke softly.

"It pleases me that you love him as I do, . . . as a brother should."

They smiled and walked quickly to the waiting boat.

FIVE

"When are we going to stand and fight?" asked Elijah as he packed some of Major Tallmadge's belongings.

"General Washington knows what he is doing, Elijah, and it's not your place to question your superior officers."

"But, Major, we gave up Long Island and retreated to New York. Then we retreated again to the Manhattan headquarters and now we run away once again to . . . where is it now? Murray Hill in Harlem Heights! Are the Redcoats going to chase us into Canada?"

"Enough! Elijah, we're not running. We're trying to use what troops we have to the best advantage and, . . . Oh! Why do I explain anything to you? Just do as you're told. I've had enough of your insubordination. Do you understand?"

"Yes, sir, I do understand, it's just that I'm anxious to . . . "

An angry glance from Tallmadge put a stop to the conversation. Elijah, grumbling to himself, went on with the packing.

*

Elijah had never seen such a grand house. The mansion of Robert Murray sat high on the hill named after its owner. The mansion also had a name. This too, was a surprise for Elijah. It was called Incelberg and was now the temporary headquarters of General George Washington and his staff. The house was so huge that all of the officers, and the general of course, were quartered there. Since Major Benjamin Tallmadge was an aide to General Washington and Elijah was orderly to the Major, Elijah had been in the mansion on many occasions. His eyes bulged wide as they gathered in the rich opulence of the decor: the hand carved doors and molding, the high ceiling, and Elijah's favorite, the enormous grand staircase which started in the center hall and curved upward for two full floors before ending on a balcony high above him.

One morning, Elijah waited outside headquarters seated on a stone bench in a small colorful garden near a bubbling fountain. He had grown accustomed to waiting. He would deliver messages from Major Tallmadge to other officers or to the major's regiment of dragoons which were nearby at a hastily put together encampment.

A bird was washing itself in the fountain and Elijah was engrossed with the splashing antics of the small, fragile creature. He didn't notice a tall, slim, flaxen-haired young man approach him. The man also watched the enticing bird. The bird continued splashing about, unperturbed by the presence of Elijah and the young man. The bird shook itself so vigorously that it fell back into the fountain. Both observers began to laugh. Elijah looked over his shoulder at the fellow bird-watcher and looked back at the bird in the water. Elijah leaped to his feet when he realized the fellow bird-watcher wore the uniform of a captain.

Elijah stood rigidly at attention and then quickly saluted. The captain, whose uniform bore the emblem of Colonel Knowlton's Rangers, was still laughing and motioned to Elijah to be at his ease. They watched the bird together again until it finally flew away.

"I'm Captain Nathan Hale. I have a letter of introduction from my commanding officer. General Washington is expecting me."

"So you're Nathan, er . . . Hale, er . . . Captain Nathan. I mean Captain Nathan Hale."

"Yes, I am. But how did anyone know to expect me in particular?"

"Oh, no. sir. No one is expecting you, but . . . well, sir, must you report immediately to the General? Do you have a few minutes?"

"I suppose so. What's this all about?"

"You'll see, sir, you'll see," said Elijah with a broad grin on his face. "Just follow me, sir."

Elijah led the young captain past the sentry guards and into the mansion/headquarters. In the center hall a sergeant stood at attention, saluted and said, "May I help you, sir?"

"He's here to see the major," said Elijah as he hurried Captain Hale toward the stairs. "This way, sir. Follow me, sir."

Captain Hale eyed his young escort with a doubting smile, but with eyes filled with curiosity as he followed Elijah up the staircase and on to the balcony. Half-way around the landing, Elijah stopped and knocked on a door.

"It's Private Churchill, sir. I've someone here to see you, sir. Shall I bring him in?"

"Come in, Elijah," said Major Tallmadge.

Elijah opened the door and entered the room. Tallmadge was seated at a writing desk with his back to the door. Busy with quill and ink, he was writing notes to his officers. "Be with you in a moment."

"Take all the time you want, Benjamin," said Captain Hale after realizing that Private Churchill had brought him to see his long-time friend and classmate.

Benjamin recognized his friend's voice and before turning around said, "Nathan, is it really you?" He leaped from his chair with a yell and the two embraced, clapping each other on their backs and jumping around the room. Elijah smiled with happiness and remembered William Tallmadge and how he had described the meeting with his brother. Closing his eyes he said a silent prayer that Will was well and had recovered from his wounds.

After the commotion of their gregarious welcome, both Benjamin and Nathan flopped down on a couple of chairs and just looked at each other.

"I see that you're with Knowlton's Rangers," said Benjamin. "That regiment was moved back into Connecticut. How does it come about that you're here? Do you carry a message from Knowlton?"

"Well, not so much a message as a letter of introduction. General Washington is expecting me."

"Washington expecting you? Knowlton? Oh, no my friend, don't tell me that you . . . Have you volunteered to become a spy for the Continental Army?"

"I can think of no greater duty. Benjamin, you know from my letter of some months ago, that I've done nothing for my country worthy of merit. I joined the army, it's fourteen months now, and that's all I've accomplished, just that, joining the army. When this opportunity arose, I took it. It's as simple as that."

With Nathan's eyes following him, Benjamin paced the room. He circled his friend and came to a stop in front of him. His expression was stern as he spoke.

"Nothing is as simple as that. You know nothing of what it takes to become a spy. Look at you. You'd stand out in a crowd. Nothing is common or ordinary about you. Your height, your hair, and you don't look well. And, might I add, you still have those ghastly white powder burns on your face from when that musket misfired. You also wrote in that same letter that you were ill. No! You cannot do this!"

"Benjamin, it's done. Just wish me well and take me to General Washington."

Tallmadge looked at his friend and realized that he could not change his mind. Taking a deep breath and letting it out in exasperation he stood, put on his coat, and with a comical bow motioned his friend to the door.

*

General Washington greeted Captain Hale warmly and after reading Colonel Knowlton's letter, he looked for a long time at the young officer.

"Captain Hale, we dearly need information as to the position, strength, and intended movements of the enemy. We lost many men on Long Island because of a lack of that type of intelligence.

And I need to know quickly. Are you aware of the dangers of this mission?"

"I do, sir. On my honor, you'll have that information or I'll die getting it!"

The general smiled and the warmth of that smile told Captain Hale how this man held an underpaid, underfed, and impoverished army together.

"That information will save lives Captain, but please be careful. Have you formulated a plan?"

"Yes, I have, sir."

"Excuse me, General," said Tallmadge. "Captain Hale has not fully recovered from a recent illness and has no training what-so-ever for this mission. If I may, sir, I volunteer to get the information for you."

"You did volunteer once before and were told, Benjamin, that I need your expertise here. No, I think Captain Hale will do very nicely. As for training, how many of our young men are trained for what they must do in war?"

"General, sir," said Captain Hale. "Please try to understand my friend's motives, sir. We've been friends for many years. We were classmates at Yale. We graduated together. We're as close as brothers and he wishes to protect me from unknown dangers."

"I understand, Nathan, but that changes nothing. We are all brothers in our cause. Now let me hear your plan."

"I intend to go from here to Connecticut and then cross the Sound back into Long Island, by let's say, Huntington. Then I'll move west behind the enemy. I'll disguise myself as a teacher, which I am or was before the war, and mingle with the enemy to gain the information you need."

"It's too simple," said Benjamin.

"Sometimes simple is the best way," said Nathan.

"I agree," said the general. When can you leave?"

"Immediately, sir."

"May God go with you," said General Washington.

"I wish I could," said Benjamin. The general escorted the men to the door as the three of them laughed over Benjamin's comment.

"Godspeed, Captain Hale. Get me the information that I need so desperately."

"Today is the seventeenth. I'll have that information for you in about five days. Let us say by the twenty-second of September."

The officers saluted General Washington and left the room. The two friends walked around the balcony and down the stairway. It did not go unnoticed by either of them that a youthful private had fallen into stride and was walking behind them. Benjamin did not try to dissuade Nathan any longer as, after all, he was now under direct orders from the commander-in- chief of the Continental Army.

*

The days passed slowly for Benjamin. The skirmishes at Harlem Heights secured no advantage for either side. General Washington had again been surprised and the need for critical information was amplified. The information that Nathan was obtaining was vital. The day that Nathan said he would return, the twenty-second, had come and gone. Benjamin was worried.

On the morning of the twenty-third, Benjamin Tallmadge was having coffee with Captain Hamilton when other officers came to them with news of General Nathaniel Woodhull.

"I can't believe that the English could be that cruel."

"After all, he was an officer."

"Who are you speaking of?" asked Captain Hamilton.

"General Nathaniel Woodhull. He's dead. The damn Redcoats killed him. He was their prisoner and they killed him."

"What happened?" asked Benjamin.

"He was in charge of driving all of the livestock east on Long Island to keep them away from the British. He did manage to get most of them hidden out past mid-island but then he was captured. The English officers assured him that he would be treated

as a gentleman. Then and only then did he relinquish his sword. I
was told that a British officer ordered him to say 'God save the
King'. When General Woodhull replied, 'God save us all', the
British officer struck him down with his own sword. The general,
... he's an old man you know ... put up his arm to protect
himself and had seven saber cuts on his arm and three on his head.
He eventually died of those wounds."

"He was a good man."

"May God have mercy on his soul."

"I knew the man," said Tallmadge. "He was related to a neighbor in Setauket."

After the officers finished their coffee, Tallmadge went off by
himself sickened by the horrors of war. He walked alone in the
gardens by the mansion. He found a peaceful area where the aroma
of the flowers was exceptionally sweet. There he found a deep pool
of water fed by a small stream. The shade trees provided a coolness
to the area, protecting it from the heat of the day. On a large rock
near the pool, he sat and rested. He felt apart from the war, apart
from the world and it was there that he thought of his brother.
Was he well? Was he still alive? Yes, he must be. Would he know?
If someone as close as a brother dies, can you feel it? Tallmadge
shook himself, trying to shake off the thoughts of death and dying. Why hasn't Nathan returned? He's just late. He'll be here
today or tomorrow by the latest.

A bird sang sweetly in the trees. Tallmadge searched the
branches with his eyes but the bird remained elusive. He hated to
tear himself away from the peace he felt by the shady pool, but a
staff meeting had been called for the mid- morning. He rose and
took a slow walk around the garden promising himself to return
whenever he could.

He heard his name being called. It was Elijah.

"Major Tallmadge, sir. They sent me to find you."

"Has the general moved up the time of the meeting?"

"I don't know, sir, but you're to report to the main room of the
mansion."

"It must be, yes, it's got to be. Nathan is back!"

Benjamin Tallmadge broke into a run toward the mansion with Elijah at his heels. He was elated to know that his friend, Nathan had returned safely. He entered the mansion and could not contain himself. He called out. "Nathan, Nathan my friend."

Quite unlike himself, Tallmadge burst into the staff meeting only to be greeted by a somber general and an equally somber group of officers. Tallmadge thought that their attitude was due to his outburst.

"My apologies gentlemen, my conduct is unforgivable."

General Washington approached Benjamin and placed a strong hand upon his shoulder. He spoke softly.

"Benjamin, we have just received word that Captain Nathan Hale was captured by the enemy as a spy."

A shudder went through Benjamin. He opened his mouth to speak, but could not find the words.

"I know he was your closest friend. I wanted to be the one to tell you that he . . . "

"They won't harm him. Tell me they won't harm him!"

"Benjamin, they . . . they hung him yesterday. I'm sorry."

Benjamin's eyes flooded over as he shook his head not wanting to hear, not wanting to know, not wanting to believe. He felt a sudden weakness in his legs. Washington held him up by his shoulders.

"I'm, . . . I'm all right, sir. It was just the shock. I'll be fine, sir. Thank you."

The room was silent. Benjamin looked toward the windows, but could only see a blur of light. The General continued.

"It was also reported that his last words were, 'I only regret that I have but one life to lose for my country'."

Benjamin looked at General Washington and said in Latin, *"Duice et decorum est pro patria mori."*

"What was that, Benjamin?" asked General Washington.

"Before Nathan joined the army he spoke those words to me. It is a quote from Horace and it means; 'Sweet and fitting is death for one's country'. So you see, sir, he began and ended his military career with the same thought."

"Would you like some time to yourself, Benjamin? I can delay the meeting."

"Thank you, sir, but no. There will be time enough for mourning after we win this war."

Elijah, who had been standing at the partially opened door of the meeting room, slowly closed it. He leaned against the wall and closed his eyes very tightly.

*

The meeting was long. A light dinner was sent in for the officers. By the time the meeting ended the moon had risen. Benjamin Tallmadge stepped outside the mansion and stared at the moon for a while and then looked about for Elijah. Elijah usually waited by the door or nearby, but tonight he was not around. Tallmadge turned back toward the house to go to his room when suddenly he heard someone crying. He followed the sounds and there in the little garden by the fountain he found Elijah sitting on the rock bench sobbing uncontrollably.

"Elijah, what is it, boy? Why are you crying?"

"It's nothing, sir," said Elijah wiping his tears and trying to gain control of himself. He was embarrassed that the major had seen him in such a wretched state.

"What is it, Elijah? Get a hold on yourself."

"Then . . . you haven't heard? I . . . I just spoke with one of the men who had been held prisoner by the British. Somehow he escaped. He told me they keep the prisoners on stripped down warships in New York Harbor. He was on the *Jersey*. It's a rat infested, filthy hole where the men are left to rot."

"Yes, I know of these ships. They're disgusting, but that's part of the horror of war. And you should know that by now. Why are you . . . ?"

"You don't understand, you don't understand," said Elijah

between sobs. "Will, your brother, was on that ship. The English didn't treat his wounds, they didn't feed him. The rats fed off his wounds. This man knew William. They let him die on that stinking ship. They let him die. William is dead."

"Agghhhhhhhhhhh." A tortured scream of disbelief exploded from Benjamin. "No, not my brother, not William." Benjamin's hands flew to his face and then to his eyes, trying to stop the pain in his head and in his heart. He ran from the garden with Elijah following. He stopped abruptly and wheeled about and faced Elijah.

"Leave me, boy. I must be alone." He turned again and strode off into the night.

How long he walked he didn't know, but he eventually found himself back at the peaceful area where he had rested earlier that morning. The moonlight cast an eerie glow on the deep pool and it fit his mood. Unknown to him, Elijah had followed. He was just outside the clearing and could see and hear Tallmadge. Benjamin was talking out loud.

"And Lord, please take the souls of my brother William and my friend, Nathan, and keep them close to you. As for me," said Tallmadge. He drew his sword from its scabbard. Elijah, thinking Tallmadge might harm himself, moved closer to stop him. But Tallmadge held the blade before him as if it were a cross. The moonlight reflected from the sword making it appear to glow in the dim light of the night. He was taking an oath on his sword!

"As for me, I am determined to die before dishonor. I will avenge the death of William and Nathan. I will serve my country well so that liberty can flourish in this sweet land. For God and Country! For Washington and Glory!"

SIX

It was early and the sun was just beginning to peek over the horizon. The night chill still lingered in the air and the heavy humidity of the night hung like wet sheets. A mounted regiment of dragoons stood silently on a hill near the mansion. The grass and low shrubs shimmered silvery with dew. The leaves of the trees dripped moisture. Silence predominated the moment. Even the birds were not yet stirring. Occasionally one of the horses would snort or impatiently pound the ground with a hoof. Feathery plumes of mist from their nostrils gave them a mystical appearance. The day was arising from slumber, patiently waiting for the sun to infuse it with new life.

The dragoons were patiently waiting also. Waiting for their commander, Major Benjamin Tallmadge. Elijah, close to the front of the regiment, turned in his saddle and stretched himself trying to see if the major was coming. Elijah was allowed that position in the regiment because he was the major's orderly. Tallmadge finally approached, walking his highly spirited black charger along the line of mounted dragoons from the rear of the regiment. He greeted his men warmly and they responded in an equally friendly manner. He was extremely well-liked and respected by his men. Most of them were older than their commander, but he had earned their respect and his youth had not deterred their feelings.

As Major Tallmadge passed Elijah he saw that the boy's attitude was very solemn and grim. He grabbed the halter of Elijah's horse and led him a short distance away.

"Elijah. Yesterday was yesterday and today is today. Just as that sunrise brings the promise of the future, we must not linger in the past. We should keep the memories of those we have lost in our hearts and never lose sight of the fact that they died for the same cause for which we must now live. General Washington said in his proclamation to this very army . . . "The fate of unborn millions will now depend on the courage and conduct of this army. We have therefore resolved to conquer or die." . . . We cannot let our friends and brothers die in vain."

"I understand, sir, said Elijah. "And thank you for talking to me as you have. Like I was part of the family."

"Yes, I do feel as though you are 'family', but you are also a private. Now, get back in line, soldier," said the Major smiling as warmly as the sun which now spread its golden glow over a new day.

"Are we riding out to attack the enemy?" asked Elijah.

Major Tallmadge though awhile as to whether he should answer the boy or not, then without a smile he said, "We are retreating to White Plains."

Elijah looked at the Major and turning his horse back to the regiment said simply, Yes, sir." He looked back at the major and his smile told Tallmadge that he did indeed understand what he had been told.

Major Tallmadge gave orders to his sergeant to move the dragoons.

"Sergeant Kanfert."

"Yes, sir, Major Tallmadge."

"Move them out, Sergeant."

"Yes, sir, Major."

At a command from the Sergeant that seemed more like a series of inflections between grunts and growls, the regiment proceeded in an orderly fashion toward the north. As they rode they began singing a romantic company song they had picked-up from a company of Minute-Men from Jamaica, Long Island.

Arouse, my brother Minute Men!

And let us hear our chorus,

The braver and the bolder,

The more they will adore us.

Our Country calls for swords and balls,
Our drums aloud do rattle,
Our fifer's charms arouse to arms,
And Liberty calls to battle.

Major Tallmadge waited on his impatiently prancing horse, until all of his men had passed before him, and then with very little encouragement, his horse galloped past the regiment and the major took his place at the head of his command.

SEVEN

In White Plains General Washington had no time to build tough defensive fortifications as the enemy was quick to follow his retreat from Harlem Heights. Instead he ordered cornstalks bunched up, set up on end and covered with earth. These sham fortifications looked quite strong. Washington was counting on General Howe, the English commander, to continue his fool-hardy ways of not attacking when and where he should. Howe seemingly had no stomach to attack American fortifications.

But General Howe did the unexpected once again. In a fierce frontal attack designed to capture Washington, he over-ran the weak fortifications. The Americans retreated. This time only five miles north to North Castle. They dug themselves into the hills and after only one attempt to dislodge them, General Howe, again doing the unexpected, simply quit.

That night General Washington called his officers to a meeting. As the officers gathered together in Washington's tent, they were silent. Their mood was somber and extremely concerned. General Washington was the last to join them. He entered quickly from the rear of the tent with Major Benjamin Tallmadge and Captain Alexander Hamilton. The General surveyed his officers before beginning to speak.

"Gentlemen, if the enemy launches an attack similar to their initial attempt at White Plains, we may not be able to successfully defend ourselves. It would be equally futile for us to stay in our present position as I have information that General Carleton is coming from Canada to join Howe. Our own General Arnold is slowing Carleton's movements enough so that we can cross to New Jersey and stay at least a day's march ahead of the enemy. I also have information that Cornwallis is bringing an enemy force up from New York to attack Forts Lee and Washington. I have ordered the evacuation of both forts which have insufficient men for a proper defense."

"Sir," asked one of the officers. "Are we to continue to flee before the enemy like scared rabbits?" A rumble of agreement came from most of the officers.

"At this point in the war, we will neither fight nor totally run away. As long as this Continental Freedom Army exists, our cause will remain alive regardless of what territories the British control. In the least, we survive and perhaps we can lull the enemy into a false security. They already feel that they can destroy us at will. Our evasive procedures must frustrate them."

"Sir," said another officer. "Our men are frustrated as well. We lack supplies, many are sick and still others desert. We are a proud people and would rather die than turn tail and run."

"If we stand and fight at this time, we will surely die. When we die, so dies our cause. Yes, we're a proud people. That is why we have chosen to drink from the cup of freedom. That is why we have declared ourselves independent. That is why we have armed ourselves to fight for our rights, and that is why we will retreat across the Hudson River into New Jersey. We leave at once! That is all, gentlemen."

An angry General stood silently as his officers filed out of the tent. When the last had left he sat wearily in a chair and stared into space. Major Tallmadge, who had stayed behind, cleared his throat, reminding the General that he was still in the tent. The general looked at him and took the maps Tallmadge held under his arm and spread them on the table.

"Benjamin," said Washington as he pointed to an area on the large map. "We will cross here and I hope to meet with General Greene and the supplies, here."

"General, I noticed that you mentioned that we are getting some information about the enemy. How do we come by this intelligence?"

"General Scott has some isolated sources which have been helpful. I've asked him to continue gathering such information and forwarding it to me when he can."

"I have an idea that I've been working on, that may bring us more, if not all of the information we need. If I may discuss . . . "

"Keep working on it, Benjamin, and yes, I'll discuss it with you, but not now. Right now we have to move what's left of this army across the Hudson."

*

Howe chased Washington's army throughout November and into December. They moved southwest across New Jersey. General Washington kept just ahead of them, moving only when they moved, stopping when they stopped. If the English moved back toward New York, Washington followed them. This angered them and caused great anguish among the British officers. The British felt it was almost impossible to catch them and by mid-December, after they had driven the continental army into Pennsylvania, the English decided that the campaign was over for the winter. Generals Howe and Cornwallis took their troops back to New York and Long Island. Carleton, sufficiently delayed by General Arnold, had gone back to Canada. The only garrisons remaining in New Jersey were in Trenton and Princeton, with supplies in Bordentown and New Brunswick. The English were sure that the small American army would be diminished by cold and starvation and would easily be destroyed in the spring. They settled down for a comfortable winter in New York and Long Island.

The English were living in comfort, billeted in some of the homes of the very soldiers who were freezing and starving in Pennsylvania. Christmas was drawing near and the men thought of their families and of happier times.

Elijah dreamed of this mother and his brother and sister. He even remembered the pleasant times with his father. They'd have roast goose for Christmas dinner with all the trimmings including candied sweet potatoes, which were his favorite. He could see and almost smell the beautifully set table and picture himself eating his fill in the warm cozy kitchen of his family's ranch house. Later he would spend hours by the fire and perhaps his mother would call him for a snack. Yes, she would call him, most definitely she would call him. He could hear her now, calling Elijah, Elijah . . . .

"Elijah! Are you deaf, boy? I've been calling you, . . . oh, I startled you. I'm sorry." It was then that Benjamin took a good look at Elijah. "Are you well?" he asked.

"Yes, sir. I was just day-dreaming of, . . . well, . . . of home. My home at Christmas time. I've never been away and . . . I was just thinking."

"I understand, Elijah." Tallmadge looked at the boy and wanted to say more, but the words would not come. He put his arm on the boy's shoulders and pulled a folded paper from his pocket. He said, "General Washington has asked all officers to read this to our men. Perhaps I can give you a private reading before I speak to the dragoons. It's a pamphlet written by a man called Thomas Paine. He's an editor for a Pennsylvania magazine. He wrote this, it seems, just for us. He calls it, *The American Crisis*. This is what he says:

"These are the times that try men's souls. The summer soldier and the sunshine patriot will, in this crisis, shrink from the service of their country; but he that stands it now deserves the love and thanks of man and woman.

Tyranny, like hell, is not easily conquered."

Major Tallmadge read on and completed the short pamphlet. Elijah was up-lifted in spirit. He and the other soldiers in the brave Continental American Army were praised and honored. The Major smiled as he finished reading and then said, "The people do know what's happening and that we are here. The fight for freedom is alive and well and growing strong in the hearts of our fellow patriots."

"It sort of makes us, er, you know, like heroes. Even though we may starve or freeze to death on Christmas Day, I'm glad he wrote it. It makes me feel . . . . worthwhile," said Elijah.

"Keep that positive thought and a hopeful heart, my young friend, and Christmas may be a surprise for you. It certainly will be one Christmas that you will never forget."

EIGHT

The preparations took most of Christmas day, but by early evening twenty-four hundred men were slowly moving down the treacherous slopes to the banks of the Delaware River. The dragoons were taking special care with their horses. It had been snowing and raining throughout the day and now as they attempted the most dangerous portion of their journey, the weather had worsened. The rain gave way to freezing rain and sleet and the snow started to reach storm proportions. Each dragoon took delicate care in walking his horse down the steep embankment. They spoke gently to their animals and the softness of their voices gave the horses confidence. Elijah walked backwards as he led his mare. He kept a run-on conversation with her. The trails became muddy as the weight of more and more men and horses continued down toward the river. The mud made the incline more treacherous for man and horse. Many a horse's legs became rigid as they leaned back and slid, their tails slicing through the cold mud.

Elijah tried to move his horse sideways off the trail where the footing might be better. He and the other dragoons were fearful the delicate ankles of the horses would snap if a hoof became lodged in a crevice or wedged between rocks. No veterinarians had been included in this army.

When the dragoons and their horses reached the level area which continued to the river's edge, a new problem arose. The smooth river rocks were encrusted with frozen sleet and snow. The footing was dangerous. Horse and man would step onto what appeared to be firm rock, only to feel the crusted surface give way. Feet and hooves would slide to positions which were unintentional on first placement. The front leg of Elijah's mare slid into a crevice which would have fractured her ankle if Elijah had not calmed the frightened animal and gently lifted the endangered leg up and out.

The dragoons and their horses proceeded slowly to the bank of the river where they would be loaded on barges for the crossing. A few of the men fell, cursing the slippery rocks. With the exception of a few bumps and bruises, all of the men and horses made it to the waiting area. Major Tallmadge left his black stallion with Elijah and told him where to meet him after both animals were safely loaded aboard a barge.

Standing still, Elijah became painfully aware of the extreme cold. He moved between the two animals to find some relief from the incessant icy wind. His legs felt numb. He stamped them just to be sure he could. The frozen sleet came off his trousers and fell like splinters of glass and slithered on the frozen ground. The wind lashed snow and sleet upon his face and he constantly wiped the crusted snow and ice from his eyebrows and nose. His faced burned when he touched it. Elijah tried to get his collar higher and his hat lower. He readjusted the large scarf he felt privileged to have. Most of the men were poorly dressed for this severe winter weather. Major Tallmadge had given him the scarf and as he wrapped it around the lower portion of his face he was grateful that his superior officer was also like a big brother.

Loading the horses aboard the barge was not an easy task. Many of the animals became frightened and had to be blindfolded. The Major's highly spirited black stallion had to have his eyes covered. Elijah was proud of his mare. She walked on to the barge uneventfully without a covering for her eyes. As Elijah was leaving the barge one of the horses, which perhaps should have had a blindfold, became frightened and despite the assistance of many dragoons, the horse broke through a railing and fell into the freezing water. Elijah and the others watched helplessly as the struggling animal slipped beneath the icy fast-moving river water, its last desperate whinny cut short by the engulfing water. Elijah's eyes followed that spot on the surface of the water, but the horse never reappeared again. Elijah looked to his mare and the major's stallion. A dragoon standing near them, saw his concern and said, "They'll be just fine, boy. I'll be lookin' after 'em."

"Thank you. The black one belongs to Major Tallmadge and I wouldn't . . . "

"I know it, boy, I'll be lookin' after both of 'em. Don't you worry now."

Elijah found Major Tallmadge where he said he would be. He was busy talking with a group of officers. After Elijah made his presence known to the major, he walked to the river's edge and looked at the ice-choked river. How would we ever get across to the other side, he thought. The other side . . . Elijah strained his eyes, but could not glimpse the other bank of the river. The river was fast, but at least they were below the rapids and waterfalls which were breaking up the ice on the river and causing all of the ice floes.

When Elijah had been told that the army was finally going to attack the enemy he was elated, but now he wondered if they would live through the river crossing. Major Tallmadge had explained to him that this spot had been chosen for the crossing because, even though the river was fast moving, it was deep enough for the boats and barges and was relatively free of rocks. It was also only seven and a half miles up-river from Trenton where they would attack the enemy. This was the best spot for the west-east crossing back into New Jersey. The best spot. Elijah shuddered as he looked at the icy gray river water spotted with white ice floes. He saw one floe that looked as big as a boat. It appeared to be carrying rocks along with it. He watched it as it passed across his line of vision from left to right. He was glad that piece of danger would not be in the river when he made the crossing. He looked about for the boat that they would be using.

Major Tallmadge told him to stay by his side and that he would be in the boat with the officers. There, there it is. He moved toward the boat and examined it. It was about twenty feet long and perhaps five feet wide. Elijah was familiar with boats, but only in the summer for fishing or just plain fun. He had never been on a boat in the winter and now he was going to cross an icy river in an open boat during a severe winter storm. On closer look at the boat, which glistened under a half-inch coating of ice, one of the seats was cracked and several of the side planks were also. Elijah wondered if this boat would take them to New Jersey or to Hell.

He tried to move the boat, but besides its great weight, it was frozen to the riverbank. It would take several men to release it and move it onto the river. A shiver of cold went through him and he once again began stamping his feet, trying to keep them warm.

"Keep moving, boy. It's the only way you'll keep from freezing," said a voice from behind Elijah. He turned to see Colonel Glover and a few of his men approaching.

"Give us a hand with this boat," said the Colonel.

"Yes, sir," said Elijah eager to be useful.

The men broke the vessel free from its ice tether with a loud crack. Then they hammered at it with short thick tree branches cracking the boat free of its icy cocoon. The boat was old, but appeared quite strong and well made. Elijah was beginning to believe that this boat could make it across the Delaware.

The officers started to gather at the boat and it was pushed onto the river and moved to where the water was still and boarding would be easier. Colonel Glover and his men held the boat steady as the officers climbed aboard. Major Tallmadge motioned to Elijah to join him and together they went on board the small craft. Elijah was pleased to see that some of Colonel Glover's men were coming along. They, as experienced boatmen, were in charge of the crossing. When the boat was loaded the men sat silently and waited. The crunch of heavy footsteps in the snow caused them all to turn. There standing before them was their leader, their commander-in-chief, General Washington.

"Please gentlemen, don't stand," said Washington with a smile. Laughter arose from the small group of officers and enlisted men and the general stepped briskly onto the boat and took a forward position. He stood with one foot raised on a seat, his greatcoat over his shoulders. Raising his voice to be heard over the wind, he spoke to the officers and men on all the boats.

"Historians may someday look upon this day and our endeavors as the turning point of the war. Today we attack our enemy. I pray for victory. A victory that will show the English that we are not 'just rabble in arms' as they call us, but a formidable army who will eventually defeat them. May God look with favor upon our efforts this day. Now! On to Trenton and victory!"

"To Trenton and victory," echoed the men.

"For God and Country," said Major Tallmadge.

"And for Washington and Glory," shouted Elijah.

Tallmadge looked at Elijah and smiled. He wondered how Elijah had hit upon the very words he had used when he swore an oath upon his sword back at the Incleberg mansion in Harlem Heights.

The boat lurched forward and the men took up their oars. They propelled the boat out into the river. At a pre-arranged signal the other boats moved into the river current. Horses whinnied and stamped their hooves aboard the barges. At that moment, two thousand four hundred men, with horses, weapons, and supplies were committed to crossing the Delaware River and had placed themselves upon the mercy of the storm.

The boat moved out smartly and smoothly at first, then the main current grabbed at it and the men did all that they could do to keep the boat moving forward. Elijah kept brushing the snow from his eyes in an effort to see the eastern river bank. It was no use. The snow storm blocked his vision as the sleet lashed at his face and hands. Some time had passed before Elijah realized that General Washington was still standing. The snow and sleet sluiced down his back in the folds of this coat. He stood motionless and rigid. His face always forward and unprotected.

"Why?" asked Elijah turning toward Major Tallmadge. "Why is the general still standing?"

"He's a great leader. He knows that it's important for the men to see their leader at the front and going through what they are also enduring. He stands so that he can be seen and be an encouragement for us all."

"But, what if he were to fall?"

"I would not let him fall," said Tallmadge calmly as he looked up at his general. Elijah could see that Tallmadge had braced himself against that possibility. Just then a large ice floe rammed into the boat and it was fended off. Elijah saw Major Tallmadge move toward the general, but there was no need, Washington had not moved.

The men grew silent as more ice floes appeared. Those manning the oars strained against the current as the boats entered what Colonel Glover said was mid-river. The snow and sleet continued unabated. Some of the men started to bail the water which had accumulated on the bottom of the boat. When one man stopped and placed his freezing fingers into his mouth, Elijah picked up the cup he had dropped. He dipped the cup into the water and felt his fingers go numb. He continued bailing the ice water until he too had to drop the cup. The feeling in his hand changed from numbness to severe pain.

More and more water came into the boat and the men doubled their efforts. The ice floes were larger then before and the current much stronger. They fended off what they could and tried to soften the shock to the boat of those that could not be pushed away. Elijah kept bailing as fast as he could. He heard a cheer rise up from the men in all the boats.

"What was that?" Elijah asked.

"We can see the opposite side of the river, " said the young officer sitting next to him.

This encouraged the rowers and soon, after they had come to a lee near a bend in the river, the current abated and the ice floes lessened. Moments later the boats touched the embankment in New Jersey. A cheer once again arose from the men as they quickly disembarked and the fighting force was assembled. The officers took charge of the men in their command and they moved out in two columns toward Trenton. Major Tallmadge and his dragoons along with Elijah were in the column which followed the river. The second column took a route which would place them north of Trenton. At a pre-arranged signal, the two columns would attack the garrison at Trenton in the early dawn.

*

The storm continued through the night but the men kept up the pace set by the officers. By early morning the two columns of American warriors were in position and poised for attack. The patriotic battle cry rang out and the enemy was taken completely unaware.

Shortly after the initial charge, an officer from a Virginia regiment was shot and knocked off his horse. His boot became entangled in the stirrup and he was being dragged by his horse. Elijah went quickly to the aid of the officer. He spurred his mount onward and caught the officer's horse. He dismounted quickly, calmed the frightened animal, and then dislodged the officer's boot from the stirrup. Elijah then dragged the officer to relative safety and tended to his wound. He was surprised to see that the officer was only a little older than he was.

"Thank you, Private . . . Private?"

"Private Churchill, sir. Sir, were you hit any place beside your arm?"

"No, just the arm. It's bad enough."

"It doesn't look too bad, sir. The ball didn't hit any bone. It went clear through. May I ask your name, sir?"

"James. That is, I'm Lieutenant James Monroe from Virginia."

"I'll get the doctor, but I'd better put on a bandage to help stop the bleeding. You've lost a lot of blood already, Lieutenant Monroe."

Ripping a piece of his shirt, Elijah wrapped the officer's arm tightly enough to stop the bleeding.

"There, that should do until I find the doctor," said Elijah as he finished the make-shift bandage.

"Never mind the doctor. Help me to my horse." said Monroe as he tried to raise himself only to fall back. Elijah found the doctor and brought him to where the lieutenant lay wounded. The battle lasted less than an hour and Elijah had seen only a few minutes of fighting. The Trenton garrison was destroyed. The entire mercenary force of the Hessians was killed or captured. After the battle Elijah went to see how Lieutenant Monroe was doing.

"He'll be just fine," said the doctor.

"Were there many American casualties from the battle?" asked Elijah.

"Four were wounded, and six are dead if you count the two that froze to death on the march to get here."

"I didn't know. They must've been in the other column."

"They were weaker and had less clothing than the others. This victory does more than just give the army a big boost in ego. The food, provisions, clothing, and blankets will save lives."

Major Tallmadge rode up, his black charger wild-eyed and still excited from the battle.

"Elijah, you worried me. Where've you been?"

"Well, sir, I . . . "

"I'd best answer for him, sir," said the lieutenant. "You have one fine soldier here, Major. He saved my life. I think he should have a promotion."

The major wiped his sword clean and returned it to its scabbard. He was beaming with pride but tried not to show it.

"Yes, I'll consider a promotion for Private Churchill, but for now, Elijah," said Tallmadge as he dismounted from his steed. "I want you to help me get the Lieutenant into that wagon over there. He won't be on horseback for a while."

The Americans found the much needed supplies and munitions in Trenton. The men settled in for a good night's sleep after a full hot meal. At dinner that evening all the officers ate with General Washington. Every so often during the meal a dragoon would enter the dining room and give a message to Major Tallmadge. General Washington watched as each message was read and waited for a signal from Tallmadge. The officers were elated with their success and they spoke openly of the day's events.

".'. . . and the best of all, our men have never been in higher spirits," said one colonel.

"All of the men will re-enlist."

"Some of the local militia have already enlisted."

"Our ranks are swelling."

Washington let them talk on and on for they had been fighting for some time and they had never savored a victory. Another dragoon entered and gave a message to Benjamin. This time the major nodded to General Washington, who motioned Tallmadge to his side. They stepped out of ear shot from the others, spoke for a moment, and then Major Tallmadge left. Washington returned to the table and while still standing, asked for silence.

"Gentlemen, I asked Major Tallmadge to send out some of his dragoons to see if there was any movement from the enemy. I have a positive report that Cornwallis, with a large contingent of soldiers, is rushing from New York to engage us. We'll be outnumbered, but I have a plan. Go now and prepare your men for battle. Be prepared to march, for I've not decided where that battle will be.

*

Within the hour, Major Tallmadge mounted his black stallion and rode to his waiting dragoons.

"Be prepared to move on my command, Sergeant Kanfert."

"Yes, sir, Major Tallmadge."

"Sir," called out Elijah, "Are we retreating?"

Tallmadge stared at Elijah and then down the long line of mounted dragoons. His stallion, sensing the excitement about him, reared up and pawed the air with his hooves.

"Retreating? Hell no, Elijah! We ride to attack the English at Princeton!"

NINE

"I'm amazed, sir, that Cornwallis has not made any attempt to engage us in battle. I thought for sure that after we slipped around his army and attacked Princeton that he would hit us with everything he had. He must know of our success, our great victory at Princeton. Why does he run back to New York?" asked Major Tallmadge as he moved his horse closer to the one General Washington was riding.

Washington was leading his victorious army to some well earned rest into the hills around Morristown. Only two of his officers rode side by side with their general on this the first morning after the Princeton Victory.

"Yes, sir," said Captain Hamilton. "I too wondered why they turned tail."

"The answer is simple, Gentlemen. After our victories at Trenton and Princeton, Cornwallis must have assumed that we had more men then we actually do. I'm certain that he was fearful that we would cut him off from his supplies and perhaps notch another victory against the English."

"It's hard to believe. Only ten days ago, things looked so bleak and now, after these two quick victories, you've liberated virtually all of New Jersey. My compliments, sir, on your excellent strategy," said Hamilton.

"Your strategy has also restored the shattered morale of the men. They're in very high spirits and others are enlisting in droves. Yes, sir, you're to be complimented," said Major Tallmadge.

"Thank you, gentlemen, thank you. May I remind you that any strategy is only good if it is implemented well by fine men led by excellent officers. I've been blessed with both."

A corporal rode up to Captain Hamilton. He saluted smartly. It was obvious that he was nervous being so close to General Washington.

"Yes, Corporal, what is it?" asked Hamilton.

"Well, sir, it's the artillery we confiscated from the British. Some of it appears to be, well, not in working order and they want you to decided if we should keep it or not."

"See to this, Captain," said Washington, "if the questionable artillery can be restored to proper function, keep them. If not, see to it that the artillery can never be used by our enemy."

Captain Hamilton saluted and turning his horse, rode off to the rear of the army with the corporal.

It was a fine day. The day was cold but bright, clean, and crisp. The snow storms had passed and the landscape was pristine white. The sun glistened off the ice encased branches of the trees. Soon the warmth of the sun would melt that frigid coating and the trees would drip as if it was raining. The snow was deep and it muffled the sounds of the horses and the army at march. As Major Tallmadge rode with General Washington he thought how much this was like a simple ride with a friend. But this was not a simple ride, his country was at war to drive out an oppressor. This was a war to decide if this country was indeed independent or just a part of the British colonial empire. A noise from the army behind him jolted him back to reality.

"I've meant to ask you, Benjamin, how did you manage to get that information on Cornwallis's movements as quickly as you did?"

"Oh, that was easy, sir. I sent out a dozen of my dragoons and I positioned them at equal intervals in a ring-like fashion. The ring extended from Trenton to Staten Island, down the coast to Sandy Hook and back to Trenton. My men would be aware of any movement from New York by land, or we would also know if the enemy landed on the New Jersey shore by ship. Each dragoon would stay at his position until relieved by another dragoon. Then I sent a thirteenth dragoon to replace the first. The first moved up the ring to the next position to replace the second, and so on. The messages came to us quickly because each man would relay the message. He was replaced with a fresh man and of course, a fresh horse. Since there was always one additional man in the ring, an urgent message could be relayed directly without disturbing the ring itself."

"Simple, but ingenious, Major. My compliments to you and your dragoons."

"Thank you, sir."

"Benjamin, before we left New York, you mentioned that you had an idea, a method by which you could gather intelligence. I would like to hear about that idea."

"Well, sir," Tallmadge began, "We've been getting our information from here and there. A soldier or a citizen heard something or saw something, or we would post a rider on a road to tell us if the enemy was coming. There really has been no plan to get proper, timely, and correct information. Of course, sir, I do understand that we've been kept quite busy. My friend, Nathan Hale had the right idea, but no real plan and no assistance. The only way to get what we want is to go where the English are. To infiltrate them in their own society."

"And just how do you propose to do that?" asked Washington.

"The English have occupied all of Long Island and New York. Their officers live lavishly well in our homes. They're billeted in some of the finest homes in New York as well as on Long Island. There are many patriots who pose as loyalists just simply so they'd be allowed to live and carry on their businesses. I propose to find these patriots and enlist their services. I'd choose those who are in a position to have or gain information and others who could pass that information on to me and then on to you. The idea needs some fine honing, but I know it'll work."

"It sounds fine, Benjamin and . . . "

"Excuse me, sir, for interrupting, but if I may continue, a thought just came to me. The group of patriots would be set up so that no one person knows who the others are. Aliases would be used. In this way if one spy were captured the group would not suffer and the others could continue gathering information. The captured spy, even if released, would be replaced."

"Would these patriot-spies be set up in a ring similar to what you did with the dragoons at Trenton?"

"That could be, sir, only it would have to be a little more subtle. Sir, do I have your permission to proceed with this plan?"

"You have my permission and my blessings. Take your entire regiment of dragoons and go back to Connecticut. I feel that is close enough to New York and Long Island for your ... er ... project and I had intended to send you and your dragoons anyway, to protect the Connecticut shoreline. Somehow you must also keep track of where I am to get the information to me on a regular basis. From time to time I'll have specific requests for information.

"I understand, sir. When do you want me to leave?"

"Tomorrow morning, right after we break camp. I feel that you should have an alias as well. Think about one and let me know what it is before you leave."

"Oh, I have already, sir. In this intrigue I'll be known as John Bolton."

TEN

Time had passed quickly for Major Tallmadge, Elijah, and the regiment of dragoons. They had successfully defended the Connecticut shoreline on many occasions and Elijah was proud to have been promoted to corporal. Benjamin Tallmadge had some success in getting important troop movement information to General Washington, but his dream of setting up a ring of spies had eluded him.

It was almost a year and a half since he had promised his general a workable spy system. His failure angered and frustrated him. Although he had many letters of correspondence with General Washington, and never once had the general questioned him about it, Tallmadge felt as if he had let his general and his country down.

In the early summer Tallmadge discovered that William Townsend, who had attended Yale with him, had a brother who ran a business in the heart of New York. Both William and his brother Robert, were known as loyalists, but Tallmadge knew that William was a patriot through and through. He had to be sure that Robert shared the same feelings as his brother and if he did, would he be willing to risk everything to help the cause of freedom. How to get this information befuddled him.

Benjamin leaned back on his chair and stared out of the window of his Connecticut home. He could see Elijah and another dragoon talking in the shade of the trees by the stable. How he had grown and yet he was still a young boy. No one would ever take him for a corporal in the Second Regiment of Light Dragoons. No one would ever take him . . . "Of course!" Shouted Tallmadge as he jumped from his chair and ran to the door.

"Elijah, Elijah! Come here quickly. I must talk to you."

Tallmadge's call was so startling and commanded such urgency that Elijah abruptly broke his conversation with the other Dragoon. Half-way to the house he realized his rudeness and called back an apology to his friend who smiled and waved to him. Major Tallmadge waited for Elijah at the doorway.

"Come in Elijah," he said hurriedly.

"Sir, I . . . "

"Sit down, Elijah and just listen. I've an urgent need to go to Long Island to meet with an old friend. I, of course, cannot just go. I'm too well known, but if we were to go together, well, it could work out."

"Forgive me, sir, but you're not making any sense."

Tallmadge looked at the young dragoon and sat down. "No, I guess I'm not. First let me explain that this is not just a visit. I must see this man on a military matter. We'd be going to Oyster Bay. We'd land at night. I'd wait at the boat and you, dressed as one of the locals, could go to my friend's home, speak to him and lead him back to me.

Elijah's face lit up with excitement and he exclaimed, "Do you mean that I'd be a spy?"

"No! Well, yes . . . sort of. Perhaps it's not a good idea to send you," said the Major as he thought of his friend Nathan Hale.

"Oh, yes, sir. It's a good idea. No one would know who I am. I could pass as just some young boy. No one would know that I'm a dragoon. No harm could come to me."

Major Tallmadge smiled and he patted his eager young friend's head. He paced the room for a while in deep thought. Elijah said nothing. His eyes just followed the major back and forth. Finally Benjamin stopped pacing and spoke.

"We would need a boat. Bring me the best of the whaleboat captains. Ask the rest of the dragoons who that might be."

"I don't have to ask," said Elijah jumping up from his chair, "I already know. It's Caleb Brewster! Perhaps you already know him. He's from our village . . . Setauket."

"Caleb is a whaleboat captain? I do know him, but I didn't

know that he was one of the whaleboat warriors, those will-o-the-wisps who seem to fly across the Devil's Belt and strike at the English and then fly away again. Caleb Brewster. You know, it's just like him."

"What's the Devil's Belt, sir?"

"It's an old sailor's name for the Long Island Sound. Now, go find Caleb Brewster and tell him that I wish to speak to him."

"Yes, sir, Major," said Elijah as he burst for the door.

"And, Elijah, you're to mention nothing to him or to anyone of what I've told you today. In fact, from now on, do not tell anyone what I say or do. If you're to be of assistance to me, you must be secretive. Do you understand?"

"Yes, sir, I understand and thank you for your faith in me."

*

Later that evening there was a knock at his door and Benjamin Tallmadge went to answer. He smiled as Elijah escorted into the room a huge man with a large toothy grin for a smile. He had a ruddy complexion acquired from years as a seafaring man. His big hands reached out to greet the Major. His blue eyes sparkled as he shook the major's hand. This man was Caleb Brewster.

*

The night was dark even though a full moon could occasionally be seen dashing from cloud cover to cloud cover as if it were trying to hide its light from the world. The air was still and the Sound had hardly a ripple on its surface. The whaleboat cut through the night and the water with muffled oars. The surface of the water in Oyster Bay Harbor was silk-like. There were no sounds. There was no breeze. The night was holding its breath. The men lifted their sixteen foot oars from the water and Caleb Brewster guided the whaleboat to the beach with the rudder arm from the stern of the boat.

The bow of the whaleboat crunched against sand and pebbles on the shore, the sound breaking through the stillness of the night like a thunder clap. The men waited in silence once again as an owl hooted at their intrusion into his night. The oarsmen stepped out and held the twenty five foot boat steady as Elijah and Benjamin stepped on to the beach.

"It's best that I wait off-shore. Then I can move quickly if need be. Hoot like an owl three times and I'll come for you." said Brewster.

"We may be an hour or two," said Tallmadge.

"I'll be here, waiting . . . you can be sure."

The whaleboat and crew moved away from the beach as Elijah and the Major ran quickly across the exposed beach to a stand of jack pines silhouetted against the sky and from there to the heavily wooded area between the beach and the village. Elijah looked back to the bay. He could no longer see the boat, but he knew it was there. The two stayed off the paths and eventually came to the edge of town.

"This is as far as I dare go," said Tallmadge in a whisper. "Go straight to the Townsend house along the roads we spoke of and remember, you're out of uniform so if you're captured, well, you . . ."

"Don't worry, sir. I'll be back as soon as I can."

Elijah stepped out from the blackness of the trees and walked to the center of the road. As planned he walked causally, but with direction, as if he were walking in his own home town and it was not occupied by the enemy.

The roads of the town were empty and many of the houses were in darkness. Elijah saw the flickering glow of candles, and the stronger warm light from the parlor hearths through the windows of most of the houses. He found the Townsend house without any problem and it was well lighted as if a party was going on. Through the windows, into the well-lighted rooms, Elijah could see several people. He decided to go to the back door. He walked through the garden gate. Passing a gazebo, he approached the steps to the back door. He realized too late that he was not alone. Three men stepped from the shadows by the gazebo. They were in uniform and they were Redcoats.

Elijah froze as they approached him. He suppressed the urge to run. His mind was racing. He was trying to remember what to say to them. Major Tallmadge told him what to do under any possible circumstance. He had been told what to say if approached by Redcoats, but his mind had gone blank.

"What 'ave we 'ere?" asked one of the soldiers.

"Yes, boy, why do you approach the rear of this home? All expected and welcomed guests use the front door," said another.

Elijah still could not speak. He hoped that he did not look as frightened as he felt.

"Perhaps 'e's a little of both, welcome to some and not to others? Is that it, boy?"

"Well, sort of . . . ," said Elijah trying to manage a smile.

"I think 'e's a boyfriend of that pretty young thing what lives 'ere."

The three Redcoats laughed and grabbed him roughly. It became obvious to Elijah that they had been drinking heavily.

"Come on, boy," said one them as they pulled him toward the back door, "We'll show you 'ow to be a proper suitor." They laughed again and banged on the door.

"What's your girl's name, boy?"

Elijah stared at the soldier with his mouth open.

"What's 'er name?" he repeated, this time without laughter and without a smile.

Even though Elijah made no move to run they held him more firmly than before.

"Speak up, boy. If you don't know your girlfriend's name, perhaps our Colonel would like to meet you!"

Elijah knew that it was all over. Perhaps if he said nothing at all he might get by, but if he were brought to the officers, for sure they would see through his facade.

"I think you should meet our Colonel!"

"What's the trouble out here?" asked a pretty young girl of about Elijah's age. "Who do you have out there?" She strained her eyes to see into the darkened area where the Soldiers held Elijah. She stepped outside and the Redcoats brought Elijah into the light.

"You know this bloke, Miss Townsend?" They held and pushed Elijah's face toward the girl.

Sally Townsend studied Elijah's face for a moment and said, "James, what trouble have you gotten yourself into now?"

"You know 'em, Miss?" said one of the Redcoats as they released Elijah.

"Of course I do, I told him to come and visit me, but James, I expected you an hour ago," said Sally as she took Elijah's arm and led him into the house.

Elijah just smiled at her and looking back at the Redcoats, he entered the house. He followed Sally Townsend through the cooking area into a small utility room used for the storage of pots, pans, eating utensils, glassware, and fine china. She spoke to Elijah quietly, but he noticed a touch of fear in her voice.

"Who are you and what do you want here?"

"Please have no fear of me. My name is Elijah Churchill and please pray tell, before someone else asks me, what is your name? I heard one of the guards call you Miss Townsend, but what is your given name?"

"My name is Sarah, but everyone calls me Sally. I want to know what you're doing here. I can still call those guards."

"Thank you for helping me. Why did you? You don't know me at all."

"You had such concern in your eyes. Your eyes were pleading with me to help you. I could feel that the soldiers were your enemy."

"That was fear in my eyes, not concern. Are they your enemy as well?" asked Elijah with a smile.

Sally studied him slowly and then said, "Once again now, and this time I want an answer. If you do not tell me I'll scream and that scream will bring my family and the soldiers. Now, ... "

"Yes, I know. What am I doing here? I must speak with your brother, William. Is he at home?"

"What do you want with my brother?"

"I can't tell you that."

Sally mulled her thoughts, wondering what to do. Although she had just met Elijah, and he was acting mysteriously, she liked him and was inclined to trust him.

"Wait here," she said.

"And where would I go?" said Elijah with a big grin.

A few minutes later Sally returned with two men. The taller of the two closed the door behind him and approached Elijah. Both men said nothing as they stood one to either side of him. It was Sally who spoke first.

"He said his name is Elijah Churchill."

"Which of you is William Townsend?" asked Elijah.

"I am," said the shorter fair-haired man.

"I must speak to you in private, sir."

"Anything you must say to me can be said in front of my brother and sister."

"I have a message, sir, which is best told to you in private. The message is from Benjamin Tallmadge."

At the mention of the name, Benjamin Tallmadge, William moved to the window and looked out. He turned and spoke to Elijah.

"You endanger all of us by coming here. Sally, Robert, please wait outside the door for me."

"Oh, sir, if this man is your brother, Robert, he must stay as this message concerns him as well."

Sally reluctantly left the small room. The three watched her leave and closed the door behind her. The two brothers turned and looked at Elijah.

"I've been sent by Major Benjamin Tallmadge. He's under special orders from General Washington and he needs your assistance. He told me to tell you that he prays that although you may pose as a loyalist, your heart is that of a pure patriot, as it was at Yale. Actually, he needs your help, Robert, that is, if you have the same feelings as your brother, William. I can bring you to him and he can discuss this with you directly."

"How do we know that you are telling us the truth? This could be an English trap to test our loyalty."

William leaned against the wall in deep thought. He looked occasionally at Elijah. Both Elijah and Robert watched and waited for his answer.

"If there is any chance that it is Benjamin and that this boy is telling the truth, we must take that risk," said Robert.

"Tell us where he is," said William.

"I will lead you to him," insisted Elijah.

The two brothers nodded in agreement, but William added a warning. "We'll go with you, but we'll be armed. If this is a trap, you'll be the first to die."

"How do we get past those guards and what are they doing here?" asked Elijah.

"They're leaving, perhaps they've already done so. They were here with Colonel Simcoe of the Queens Rangers. His troops are here in Oyster Bay and he's requested permission to be lodged here in our home. It's just a formality, he can stay wherever he wishes in this town. To maintain our 'pose', as you call it, our father could not refuse."

After assuring themselves that the Redcoats had indeed left, not only the house, but the immediate area, Elijah and the Townsend brothers retraced Elijah's steps back to where Major Benjamin Tallmadge waited. Tallmadge stepped out of the shadows and extended his hand to his friend.

"Benjamin, you have no idea how glad I am that it is indeed you. I thought the boy might be leading us into a trap. How good it is to see you once again."

"I'm very glad to see you, and that boy, as young as he is, is one of my trusted dragoons. But, I asked you to come alone, William who is this man?"

"Benjamin, this is my brother, Robert. The boy, er . . . the dragoon thought that you would like to see him as well."

"I do, I do," said Tallmadge happily, "Good thinking, Elijah."

"I thought it best, sir. You'd eventually want to speak with him."

"Yes, Robert it's you I must speak with. William, I'm sorry and please forgive me, but I want to speak to your brother alone. The less you know about this the better."

"I understand, Benjamin. I'll wait over there in that thicket of trees."

Major Tallmadge waited until William was out of earshot. Then he spoke quickly and quietly to the younger brother, Robert.

"I understand that you have a business in New York that puts you in a position to hear the conversations of English officers."

"Yes, there are many who consider me their friend. I must keep up the pretense so I can continue to stay in business. You understand."

"Don't apologize, we can put that to good use. Can you gather information for us? We need intelligence on troop movements and strength, where and when they will strike, and anything else that will help the cause of freedom. I'll not lie to you. It's dangerous. If caught you'll be put to death. But, I only ask this because we must have your help."

"It goes against my nature and beliefs to be a spy, but I cannot deny my love for this country and my overriding belief in its destiny. That destiny can only be achieved through freedom for our people. Yes, Benjamin, of course I'll do what I can to help you. Finally, I can put this loyalist fraud to some use. Thank you for the chance to help. I do not fear the danger, not for myself. You give me the chance to gain back my self-respect."

"Good. Now, I cannot chance sending anyone into New York to contact you, but we must get that information out. How often do you come to visit your family here in Oyster Bay?"

"I'm only here about once a month, but I have a courier that I use to bring orders out here. He even goes as far as Setauket where he lives. Perhaps we can use him. His name is Austin Roe and I know him to be a patriot."

"Perhaps we can. I know Austin. He owns a tavern in Setauket and he definitely is a patriot. My plan isn't completely formulated. You were the key. Prepare all the information you can. I'll have it picked up here in Oyster Bay."

"I'll be here next week. It's my father's birthday."

"Next week then. I'll send Elijah. He'll have a message for you from John Bolton. From now on that's the only name you'll know me by. We must go now as others are waiting for us."

Tallmadge and Robert hurried over to William. They bid their farewells and Elijah and Tallmadge headed through the woods to the bay.

*

When Benjamin Tallmadge settled into his seat in the whaleboat he sensed a feeling of accomplishment even though the major work with all its problems was still ahead of him. Now that he had the key person in his spy ring he could formulate the balance of the plan. When they were a safe distance from shore to speak out loud, Caleb Brewster looked at him and with that big grin of his and in his very deepest voice asked, "I trust the Major met with success this fair night?"

"Yes," said Tallmadge, "I feel that we've taken a giant step forward in the cause of freedom."

"You know, Ben, you can count on me in any adventure you're planning. With me along you can always count on success because I bring luck with me. When others in the country speak of the founding fathers, they're really speaking of my fathers', fathers', father's, . . . "

"Yes, Cale, I know, but I haven't heard it in such a long time, please tell me again."

With that permanent smile upon his face, and his giant chest swelled out with pride, he stood in the boat with one foot on the gunnel and shouted to the world.

"I am Caleb Brewster, son of Benjamin, son of Daniel, son of

Nathaniel, son of Jonathan, son of William the elder Brewster of the Mayflower."

"No one can top you, Cale. Now, get us safely back to Connecticut and we'll drink a toast to you and William, the elder Brewster of the Mayflower!"

ELEVEN

The big red mongrel dog groaned as he flopped on his side by his master's feet. Benjamin Tallmadge stopped his writing and gazed at the dog. He reached down and patted the large head which rested against his foot. He stretched his arms and yawned. He had been working for hours and the basic plan for the spy ring was formulated. He needed just one more man, one additional piece to complete the puzzle of the ring. That man was due to arrive at any moment. In fact he was long overdue. Tallmadge checked his timepiece and began to worry. Stepping outside his front door a guard saluted him.

"Good evening, Private."

"Good evening, sir."

He slowly walked in the cool evening air over to the stables. It was then that he realized that the dog was walking with him.

"Thought you were sound asleep, fella." The dog wagged his tail and Tallmadge once again tried to think of a good name for him. The mongrel was found by Elijah wandering about the camp. Elijah brought the dog to the Major and he simply refused to leave.

As he and the unnamed dog slowly strolled back to the main house, three men rode up to the gate. He could tell by size alone that one of the men was Caleb Brewster. The other must be Elijah and the third had to be Abraham Woodhull, the last man needed to complete the ring. Tallmadge quickly greeted them.

"Good evening, Cale, Elijah, and you, sir, you of course must be Abraham Woodhull. I've been waiting for you."

"There was a bit of a northerly wind on the Sound. It slowed us down," said Brewster.

"Oh, don't listen to him. It was I who slowed him down. I was late getting to the boat. Yes, I'm Abraham Woodhull and you I presume are Major Benjamin Tallmadge."

Abraham Woodhull was slight in stature. He was pale and gave the appearance of being older than his years. His voice was low and shaky but his faith as a patriot was strong. His very presence at this secretive meeting attested to his desire to serve, for it went against every fiber of his being. He was a nervous, fearful man. He extended a thin trembling hand to his host.

"Thank you for coming. I should've come to you, but a meeting such as this, well it's safer surrounded by my Dragoons rather than Redcoats." All the men laughed and Tallmadge escorted Woodhull into his home.

"Elijah, you and Caleb go and get something to eat while I talk to Mr. Woodhull. Come back directly after supper. I must speak to you both, as well," said Tallmadge.

After Woodhull was settled into a comfortable chair, Tallmadge uncovered a large platter of cold mutton and some bread. He noticed Woodhull looking at the amount of food available. As he poured wine for himself and Woodhull he explained himself. "Yes, there's enough food here for both Elijah and Caleb, but I must speak to you privately. Everything will be on a need-to-know basis. There are some things that you'll not be told, and other privileged information that you know, others will not. In this way, if any one man is captured the entire spy system will not be destroyed."

"I understand," said Woodhull and raising his glass he added, "To liberty."

"To liberty and the success of the spy ring. Let me begin, I've asked you here because you are a key piece to my plan and because I know you to be a staunch patriot. Before I start, allow me to extend my condolences on the loss of your relative, Brigadier General Nathaniel Woodhull."

"Thank you. He was a brave man. It was terrible the way the English butchered him. But tell me, how can I help you and my country?"

"I've devised a method of gathering information, important information from the British in New York. The coded messages will be brought out to Setauket by courier and then taken across the sound by whaleboat to me. I'll see to it that this information gets into the proper hands. I need someone to take the information from the courier and get it to Brewster. I want you to be that man. Also if you gain any information, you'll put it into code and pass it along to Brewster."

"Will I know the courier?"

"Yes, of necessity, but it's best that we devise a method of exchange where there'll be no contact between the two of you."

"Who is the courier?" asked Woodhull.

"His name is Austin Roe."

"I know the man. He pastures his cattle on my land."

"Exactly! That's one of the reasons why you were chosen. It's best that you and Roe don't have any direct contact for the exchange. Is there a secure place . . . say where he tends his cattle, where he can leave messages?"

Abraham Woodhull thought for a while and then spoke. "There's a group of fallen trees. The cattle seem to cluster around them to get what little shade they offer. I could put a box in the ground under the largest tree. I'll cover it with leaves and branches so it won't be detected. Tell Roe what to look for. I'm sure he'll find it."

"Good. His reason for being on your property is the cattle. He could leave the messages before driving his cattle home. It'll work."

"You mentioned a code?" asked Woodhull.

"Yes, I have a basic simple code prepared. Just numbers for places or names. We'll all use an alias and all messages will be addressed to John Bolton."

"I presume that you are John Bolton," said Woodhull. "Do you have an alias for me?"

"I was thinking of the name Culper. Samuel Culper Sr."

"Senior? Is there a Junior?"

"Yes, he's our man in New York. You also have a brother-in-law in Oyster Bay, a one Amos Underhill, who also has business in New York. I've not opened that avenue of message delivery yet, and may not. I only mention it as a possible alternative. We also have an additional courier available if for any reason Roe cannot take the ride."

"You seem to have thought of everything."

"I've made some progress but this is only the beginning. I'll expand the code and tighten security, but I feel it'll work. It must work!" said Tallmadge emphatically.

Elijah and Brewster were returning and Brewster's deep booming voice heralded their arrival at the door. Tallmadge and Woodhull smiled and laughed when Tallmadge said, "If the English were deaf, he could shout the messages from New York to Setauket."

"Cale, Elijah we're ready for you now. Cale . . . just sit anywhere . . . Cale, have you thought of the best way to get the messages across the Devil's belt?"

"I have to avoid capture by the enemy and discovery by the Tories . . . "

"You've never been caught. You've always been victorious, often wounded but never caught, is what they say," said Woodhull repeating with pride the stories told in Setauket and surrounding areas.

"And I intend to stay that way although I can do without the wounds. But, it's not by accident that I've never been caught. I plan each step of each whaleboat attack. Major Tallmadge, in answer to your question, I feel that one whaleboat will suffice. I'll always keep it hidden in one of the small inlets and creeks on Strong's Neck."

"How will I know which creek or inlet the boat is in?" asked Woodhull.

There was silence in the room as each man pondered the question. After quite a while it was Elijah who tentatively said, "I have an idea."

"Speak up, Elijah," said the major.

"Since you cannot have someone just go and tell Mr. Woodhull where the boat is, we'll need some sort of a signal which can be seen from Mr. Woodhull's farm. I know the area well. From the northeast corner of your farm, sir, you can see the hill on Strong's Neck. Something, some signal could be set up."

"Well, a fire is out of the question. It would attract too much attention," said Woodhull.

"And the English would know that it's a signal. No, it must be something ordinary, something commonplace. It must go unnoticed, except by us," said Major Tallmadge.

"I know that hill," said Brewster. "When I come across into that area I can see the widow Strong, Anna, hanging her laundry on the line."

"I can see her too, from my farm," said Woodhull.

"Well then, that's settled. We'll use the hill on Strong Neck," said Tallmadge. "Does either of you know this Anna Strong? Is she Tory or patriot? Will she help us?"

"I know her. I know her well. She's a patriot and she'll help us if I ask her to," said Caleb Brewster.

"But what should we use as a signal?"

"Why not use the laundry?" said Elijah.

The three men looked at him wondering what he meant. Without waiting to be asked, Elijah went on. "I first thought of flags, but they would also attract attention. She's always hanging clothes. Let the clothing itself mean something."

"Yes, of course, our enemies would never notice," said Woodhull.

"If she hangs six white handkerchiefs or white garments of some kind, each could represent the inlet or creek I'd be in. I could send one of my men, or better still, go myself to tell her where the whaleboat waits. The first handkerchief could mean Willow Cove; the second would mean that I'm up at the north end of Strong's Neck by the big oak that was struck by lightning; the third would be Crane Neck Bend; the fourth, let me see, yes, by the shipyard in the harbor; and fifth, . . . hmmm . . . we can use Drowned Meadow. The sixth would have to be Old Man's Bay. I put in there if enemy ships are on the prowl."

"Once she knows where you are she could replace one of the white garments or handkerchiefs with something black to represent the correct inlet then ... "

"She has a black petticoat," said Caleb. His blue eyes were mischievous as he flashed his big smile.

"Cale, you are truly amazing," said Tallmadge pouring four glasses of wine. Gentleman, I give you Washington and Glory!"

"To Washington and Glory," echoed the three.

*

The Townsend house was brightly lit and the lilt of festive music carried out into the gardens and the surrounding roads. Several carriages and their drivers were waiting outside the residence. Redcoats were everywhere. The English officers were living the high-life, eating, drinking and dancing with the high society of Oyster Bay. Elijah could see officers with ranks as high as Major and Colonel. As instructed, he had arrived at the Townsend home as late as possible. Major Tallmadge thought that the young boy would be noticed less toward the end of the festivities. So far he had gone unnoticed. Elijah was more anxious about this meeting than he was about the last. He was carrying information from Major Tallmadge to Robert Townsend. Even though the messages were from a John Bolton to a Samuel Culper Jr., Elijah also carried the preliminary code, which in itself was enough to hang him.

Elijah sat in the gazebo with Sally as he waited for her brother to come to him. Although they had spoken at length, they now sat quietly in silence. Elijah couldn't take his eyes off her. He had remembered her as a pretty girl, but now in a ball gown with her hair softly falling against her shoulders, she was beautiful. Of necessity, Elijah was in common clothes. He looked shabby. He never owned anything like the finery that the men wore at the party. His uniform was the finest garment he ever owned. He wished that perhaps someday Sally would see him in the uniform of which he was so proud.

"Why are you so quiet, Elijah?"

"You're so beautiful, its hard to think when I look at you. And be careful and remember that the name is supposed to be James."

"You make me blush, El . . . er, James."

"Some day Sally, when this is all over I'd like . . . "

The back door opened and Robert Townsend stepped out and walked to the gazebo. His features were rugged with a prominent nose and chin. He had soft brooding eyes and his smile was both shy and sensitive.

"Good evening," said Robert as he sat down next to Elijah. "Sally, please wait in the shadows by the corner of the house."

Sally did as she was told and Robert waited until she was far enough away before he spoke. "You have something for me?" he asked nervously.

"Yes, sir, I do."

"Let's make the transfer quickly before someone sees us. I'm extremely nervous," said Townsend.

"You're nervous? My heart's been pounding ever since I got here."

"Where do you have the information?"

"In my shoe, sir. The major said that it was all self explanatory. He figured that we may not have time to talk."

"Take it out of your shoe and leave it on the ground. Then I'll put it in my shoe."

"The major would like any information you can get for him," said Elijah as he bent over and slipped off his shoe. "He'd like to test the system as soon as possible."

"I'll have information in two days, three at the most," said Robert as he slipped off his shoe, placed the messages inside and replaced the shoe.

"I'll tell Major Tallmadge."

"It's best you leave now," said Townsend glancing around him. "Sally will see you to the gate. I'll wait for her here. Good-bye and Godspeed."

"For Washington and Glory," whispered Elijah, but Townsend

only nodded. Elijah left quickly and went to where Sally waited near the Lilacs at the corner of the house. They walked together to the garden gate. They stopped and he studied her face before speaking.

"Sally, I hope to . . . "

"Who are you? My brothers would say nothing to me. They want me to forget that I ever met you, that you ever came to this house. But I can't."

"It's best that you do. Someday when this war is over, I, well . . . er, someday." He reached for her hand and squeezed it gently. He looked at her once again and then turned and walked away.

Sally watched him leave, gently holding her hand where Elijah had just touched it. He looked back and waved. When he was out of sight she hurried back to her brother who was waiting at the Gazebo.

"Robert, please tell me about him."

"I cannot, but if you wish to help him and me and the patriotic cause . . . never breathe a word, but if you should learn anything at all which might help our cause, tell me, but say nothing to anyone else. That's all I dare tell you and I question myself as to why I have said anything to you at all. Heed what I've said. Lives depend upon it."

TWELVE

Robert Townsend felt uneasy as he and Austin Roe loaded his large saddle bags with commodities that were needed on the east end of the Island. Robert was the owner and purchasing agent for Townsend & Company. They imported flax, sugar, molasses, teas, coffee, and sometimes rum and iron. It was Austin Roe's job to gather the orders from the east end of Long Island and deliver the goods when the orders were small enough for the large saddle bags. Since Townsend also, under his guise as a Loyalist, had dealings with the British officers, Roe was allowed to change horses at various British stop-points throughout the ride east and the westward return. In this way the British were unwitting accomplices in the Culper ring of spies.

Robert had helped load the saddle bags many times, but this time they also carried messages from Samuel Culper Jr. to John Bolton via Samuel Culper Sr.

"Don't worry, sir," said Austin Roe. "Everything will go just fine."

"I've always looked upon the exchange of horses at the check points as a blessing. Now, I worry. What if they decide to check the saddle bags?" said Townsend his brow twisted with apprehension.

"They haven't checked me for months. I know all of the soldiers at the check points. Those Redcoats even help me with the saddle and carry the bags for me."

"Yes, but this time . . . "

"This time will be like all the others. I'll not do anything to arouse suspicion. I'll be back tomorrow."

The two men left the shop by the back door and went into the stable where Townsend kept several horses. He held the heavy saddle bags as Austin picked out a horse. He chose a large mare called 'Lady'. She was his favorite. After placing a saddle on the mare, he walked her over to where Townsend stood with the saddle bags. They could hear boisterous laughter coming from the coffee shop nearby. The coffee shop was also owned by Townsend. The establishment was frequented by Redcoats and both Townsend and Roe knew that the laughter was from them.

"Godspeed, Austin," said Townsend as he watched Roe place his foot in the stirrup and mount the mare.

"I'll be back tomorrow with orders from the outlying farms," said Roe in a loud and reassuring voice. With a wave of his hat he wheeled the mare around and galloped down the street. Townsend stood silently for a long time as he listened to Lady's hooves click along the cobblestone roads. The sound of the courier's horse faded away and laughter once again arose from the cafe. Robert Townsend shuddered and returned to his shop.

*

Austin Roe traveled south to the docks in New York. He found the Brooklyn ferry waiting and quickly boarded. Settling his horse down, he was reluctant to leave her, or her saddle bags. Since it was his custom to leave the mare and sit down and enjoy a full pipe of tobacco, he did so. Nevertheless, he positioned himself so he could see if anyone went near the mare. By the time the ferry landed in Brooklyn, the sun was setting. Roe mounted again and rode off along the familiar trail. He decided to travel by way of Jamaica rather than through Flushing. By going through Jamaica he would travel across the plains of Hampstead. It was a longer route but by far the safest. The Flushing route took him through the northern coastal towns of the Island, including Oyster Bay and Huntington where many British troops were quartered. He passed through the town of Jamaica without event. He moved at a steady pace until he arrived at the plains of Hampstead, where he started to drive Lady at a hard gallop. He planned to change horses in Hampstead and push on to Setauket, and would change horses at the same check point the following day, taking Lady back into New York with him.

Lady was working up quite a lather when he caught sight of the British check point just outside Hampstead. Roe slowed his mare to a cantor and loped up to the corral where a Redcoat greeted him and grabbed Lady by the bridle.

"Good evening, Austin," said the soldier.

"And a very good evening to you, my friend. Did you pull guard duty once again? It appears to me that you're a permanent guard at this outpost."

"It appears that way to me also. We've a new officer'ere and I don't think'e likes me at all. My word, Lady is lathered up tonight. Why the rush?"

"Oh, . . . er . . . got a late start from New York and my cows are still in pasture. I don't like keeping them out there at night," said Roe as he dismounted. "I can't stay and talk either, must push on."

"I'll help you with a new mount."

"Will you see to it that Lady is walked and brushed down please?"

"Yes, certainly. I'll have one of the Jessup boys do it. They live just across the road and they're always hanging around."

"Thank you, John, I appreciate it."

Austin Roe mounted the fresh horse and was about the leave when a loud authoritative voice rang out.

"Corporal Dunworthy!" The young Redcoat snapped to attention and saluted as an equally young lieutenant approached them. "Corporal Dunworthy, who is this man and why is he able to just ride in here unchallenged and change horses?"

"Sir, my name is Austin Roe. I'm a courier for Townsend & Company of New York. The company does business with many of the British officers on the Island. I have papers of identification, sir."

"Yes, sir,'e does 'ave papers," said the corporal.

"May I see them please, Mr. Roe? And you Corporal, you will search Mr. Roe and his saddlebags thoroughly."

A shudder went through Austin as he thought of a search. He dismounted calmly, found his identification papers and handed them to the lieutenant.

"Here you are, Lieutenant? . . . Lieutenant?"

"Lieutenant Crompton."

Austin deliberately didn't watch as the corporal made a hasty search of the saddle bags, but his heart was pounding and his mind raced as thought of discovery worried him. He stayed calm as the lieutenant returned the papers to him and the corporal mumbled something about tea and coffee in the saddle bags.

"Thank you, sir," said Austin as he retrieved his papers.

"I come through here often. I hope that it'll not be a problem, sir." Austin Roe quickly mounted his horse. "I'll gladly show you my papers each time I pass through, sir."

"That will not be necessary and neither is your sarcasm, Mr. Roe, but you will stop, and the guards will search you each and every time you come to this outpost. Is that understood?"

"Yes, sir, Lieutenant Crompton. May I have your leave, sir?"

"Yes, Mr. Roe, you may be on your way."

Austin nodded, clucked to the horse and deliberately set a slow pace until he was out of sight of the British outpost. He then breathed a sigh of relief and spurred the horse to a gallop.

After passing through the Bushy Plains below Smithtown, he turned northward. This direction would take him directly to Setauket. He avoided the main roads of Brookhaven and Setauket and cut across farmlands and through wooded areas until he came to the farm of Abraham Woodhull. Going directly to where his cattle were pastured he rounded them up. Before leaving he went to the fallen trees and dismounted. He removed a small parcel from a loosely tied sack of coffee and sat down on the largest tree trunk. Reaching under the tree with his hand he found the wooded box, lifted the lid, and placed the packet of papers inside. Replacing the lid he covered the box with leaves and dirt as he had found it. He drove his cattle home with the satisfaction that his portion of the Culper Spy system was complete.

From his farm house Abraham Woodhull heard the sounds of Roe's small herd as it was rounded up and driven along the road past his house to Roe's barn a quarter of a mile away. The dust on the road had barely settled when Abraham stepped out on to his porch. He waited until the sound of Roe and his cattle could no longer be heard and the normal sounds of the night returned. Going quickly to the fallen trees he retrieved the packet. Earlier that day he had watched the hill on Strong Neck. Anna Strong had placed her black petticoat in the place of the third handkerchief on her clothes line. Woodhull knew that Caleb would be waiting by Crane Neck Bend on Strong's Neck. Although the hour was growing late, Woodhull knew that Caleb would still be waiting. He hurried to the narrow creek and there, hidden in the tall grasses was the whaleboat with Caleb Brewster and a group of armed men.

Caleb and Abraham did not speak as Woodhull handed him the packet. Caleb grinned and winked and with one quick movement turned and stepped into his boat. Like a shadow in the night the whaleboat silently glided out into the bay and disappeared in the night fog.

*

The moon came up on the Connecticut shore and high on a hill overlooking the Sound the eyes of a lone mounted dragoon searched the surface of the bay. The fog had lifted and there was no wind. Elijah had been waiting for two hours of his watch now and was prepared to wait more if necessary. He strained his eyes at the horizon. Was that something coming? Was it Caleb's whaleboat? Yes, a whaleboat . . . but still no signal. Then the signal, . . . the cry of a gull followed by the hoot of an owl. It was Brewster. Elijah returned the signal and set his horse at a gallop down to the beach. He raced along the water's edge to greet Caleb.

"Did all go well, Caleb?" he called to the boat.

"Like clockwork, boy, like clockwork, although it was a slow clock" said Caleb as he leaped from the whaleboat to the beach. "Now get this to wherever you're taking it."

Caleb handed Elijah the packet.

"After all this has been through, I have the easy part!" said Elijah.

"Yeah, that may be, but you be careful you don't trip and break your neck in the dark," shouted the laughing Caleb as Elijah raced off on horseback. Elijah heard him and laughed as he galloped along the beach.

Elijah didn't slow down at all. At full gallop he raced along the blackened roads. Several times he felt under his tunic for the packet that carried such importance for the Culper Ring. The horse's hoof beats carried in the clear night and as he rode up to the Tallmadge home where the Major himself was waiting to greet him. Tallmadge grabbed at the reins of Elijah's horse as the boy dismounted.

"Well, Elijah?" said the eager major.

Elijah reached under his tunic and withdrew the important packet. Smiling, he handed it to the Major.

"Yes!" screamed the Major. "It works. The system works!" Elated, Major Tallmadge clasped Elijah roughly on his shoulders with both hands. "It works. Yes, yes, Elijah, the system works!"

THIRTEEN

The morning air was crisp and clear. Although by the calendar spring had arrived, on this day winter was still around. A chill wind blew from the northwest making daydreams of spring simply daydreams of spring. Major Tallmadge had moved his table away from the window and closer to the warm hearth. It was his custom to do this as winter came each year, but by now if spring had been on time, his writing table would be back by the window.

Tallmadge was preparing a new code for the Culper Ring when a particularly strong gust of wind rattled the windows and doors and chill breezes entered the room. The fire flared up and Tallmadge stopped his writing. Even the old red dog, still nameless, raised his head for the moment and returned to dreams of spring and rabbit chasing. Tallmadge warmed his hands over the hearth and thought of the spy ring. Over the past twelve months the Culper Ring had become more and more successful. The information gathered proved extremely valuable to General Washington. This information allowed the general to move his troops out of harm's way and to attack when he had the advantage of surprise and/or strength. His success and the fact that the British were not able to stop the revolution quickly, caused the American armies to grow in size. The courage and bravery of the Americans was never questioned and the British knew they were at war.

A knock at the door made Tallmadge snap out his thoughts. This could be the dragoon courier from General Washington that he had been waiting for, thought Benjamin.

"Come in," said the major as he stood and turned, warming his back by the fire. The door opened and two dragoons along with a cold gust of wind entered. One of the dragoons was Elijah who hastily closed the door against the winter cold. The two saluted the major and then edged closer to the fire.

"Come closer and warm yourselves. Will spring never come?"

"It doesn't seem that way, sir," said Elijah.

"No, sir. it was warmer last month," said the other dragoon. "But, its even colder up north where Washington, er, that is, General Washington is, sir."

The dragoon was noticeably embarrassed but Major Tallmadge paid little attention to what he knew was not disrespect to the general.

"He sent this package as well as these letters, sir", said the dragoon noticeably relieved that he had not been reprimanded.

"Thank you. You must be hungry as well as cold. Go and take care of your needs. You're dismissed, Corporal."

"Yes, sir, Major Tallmadge," said the dragoon as he saluted smartly. Elijah began a salute as well but Tallmadge stopped him.

"I'd like you to stay, Sergeant Churchill."

"Sergeant? Sir, I don't understand."

"Yes it's Sergeant now. Sergeant Elijah Churchill. You certainly deserve the promotion. You've placed your life in danger on more than one occasion; those excursions to Oyster Bay, and, more recently, your part in the spy ring."

"Thank you, Major, but I've not done anything in battle to deserve ... "

"Enough said. You are now a sergeant," said Tallmadge as he opened General Washington's sealed letters. He read in silence, his eyes darting quickly from left to right across the written page. A smile broadened across his face as he hurried to finish the letter.

"Elijah, this is wonderful!" said Tallmadge as he hastily opened the sealed package from General Washington. "This will make life a little easier for the couriers of our messages."

The package contained several small bottles of different liquids. The major picked up the letter once again and reread a portion of it. After reading carefully and slowly, he placed the letter on the table and examined the phials with a reverence as though they were precious icons.

"Sir, what is that liquid? How can it help the Culpers?"

"This liquid, as unbelievable as it may sound, is an invisible ink. According to this letter from General Washington, you simply write with the liquid marked, "A" . . . that's in these bottles, and then after it dries, by the application of small amounts of this liquid marked, "B" the writing will reveal itself. I must try it. Quickly, Elijah, get me a fresh quill from that drawer please."

As Elijah went for the quill, Tallmadge prepared a sheet of paper and gently opened one of the bottles marked "A". He hesitated in thought for a moment and then dipped the quill into the liquid. He wrote on the paper and nothing appeared. He stopped, recapped the bottle of precious liquid, and waved the paper about to speed the drying. The major examined the paper and with a smile slowly handed it to Elijah.

"There's no sign of any script on this paper and yet I saw you write," said Elijah.

"Now for the important part," said Tallmadge as he retrieved the paper from Elijah.

Opening one of the bottles marked, "B" he gently touched the tip of the feathery end of the quill into the liquid. As he lightly brushed the dampened feather across the paper in the area where he had written, his writing reappeared. He again dried the paper and handed it to Elijah.

"It says, "For Washington and Glory". I can read it and nothing was visible before. This is wonderful! . . . A secret stain."

"Yes, an invisible stain."

"Now the couriers need not worry about the messages they carry. The Redcoats will just find blank pieces of paper," said Elijah.

"Blank pieces of paper. Hmmmmm. That will still attract attention, perhaps even more so."

"What if a lot of blank paper were carried?" said Elijah. The magical powers of the ink had excited him and he could hardly contain himself. "Then . . . then the one sheet of blank paper would go unnoticed."

"Austin doesn't usually carry large quantities of paper. If he were to do so now, that would attract attention and how would we know which paper carried the message? We would have to mark it somehow and that would set it apart from the other paper and arouse suspicion. The British aren't fools, you know," said Tallmadge as he started to pace the floor.

"I understand, sir. The message must look ordinary and usual."

"Yes, boy, ordinary and usual. Something he would be expected to carry."

"How about a letter from Austin's family or his wife? The message could be written, with the special stain, between the lines of the personal letter."

"Yes, Elijah, I think you've hit upon it, but not a letter from home or from his wife. He'd have to have many, sometimes three or four a week. No. Samuel Culper Jr. will begin a correspondence with a customer. It'll be quite natural for a well known Tory businessman to write to a well known Tory customer. Of course Roe, and the other courier we sometimes use, Jonas Hawkins, must be sure that these letters never get to whoever they will be addressed to."

"I've never met Austin Roe. He has to be a special kind of man," said Elijah.

"All of the Culpers are special. But yes, I know what you mean. He makes that dangerous fifty-five mile journey on horseback, several times each week. Besides the Redcoats, there are the highway men. What are they called? Cowboys? That group that knows no flag or allegiance and plunders both sides to line their own greedy pockets."

"Yes, sir, they're called Cowboys. Cale Brewster hates them. He's made several raids against them. Whenever he finds out where they're camped he hits them hard. Are they bothering the Culper couriers as well?"

"So far we've been able to avoid them. I hear from Samuel Culper Sr. that Austin has had near encounters with them. Yes,

Elijah boy, Austin Roe is special. Boston has its Paul Revere and he too is to be praised. He made that ride to warn the Boston patriots that the British were on their way. Austin makes many rides each week through British occupied territory carrying messages as a spy. Capture would mean death for that brave man. I pray that the Culpers will be spared. Each risks so much that our country can be free of English oppression. May God smile upon these good men and women and keep them safe. Tallmadge sat down at his desk and began writing. Finishing the letter he picked up the quill he used for the special stain and began to write between the lines of the first letter.

"Elijah," said the major looking up from his desk. "Tell Cale Brewster to ready one of his whaleboats. We have a message and a package that we'll send in reverse of the usual pattern. And also tell Captain Brewster that I wish to speak with him today before he leaves for the Island. I want to personally give him the prepared messages and packages for the Culpers."

*

It was dusk by the time Elijah finally located Caleb Brewster and accompanied him back to the Tallmadge home. Since it was past the supper hour and neither of them had eaten, the major ordered food and the three discussed the war in general and the Culper Ring in particular.

"The evening grows late," said the major.

"The later the better for crossing the Devil's Belt," said Brewster finishing his third pint of wine. "The British sentries fall asleep when they know their officers aren't about. And the officers? They're sleeping!" He slapped the table with an open hand the size of a saddle bag and the three men laughed.

"Cale, how are you able to hold so much wine? I'd be asleep just like the British officers if I drank as much as you."

"And I'd be sick or dead," said Elijah holding his stomach and mouth. The laughter continued.

"Late enough or not, I want this to get to the Island before the courier leaves in the morning," said Tallmadge as he handed Brewster two packages.

"May I go too, sir? Cale . . . er . . . that is, Captain Brewster said he'd show me how to use the swivel gun he has mounted on the bow of his whale boat.

"Yes you may. You can also report back to me in the morning. I wish to hear of the success of the mission."

"Remember, boy, we go to Setauket. No stop over in Oyster Bay to see that pretty young thing you're sweet on," said Brewster.

Elijah didn't answer, but his face turned crimson red which set the other two men laughing once again. Elijah, sensing his blush laughed with them.

Major Tallmadge walked with Elijah and Cale Brewster to the door. They were still laughing, but when Tallmadge handed Brewster the packages their mood quickly changed and became serious.

"This may very well be the single most important night for the Culper Ring and indeed for the success of our cause. We're in a secret service to General Washington and our future success may very well depend upon these packages. Godspeed my friends. Each crossing is dangerous for many reasons. Be careful and if capture is eminent, destroy the contents of this package!"

*

The Devil's belt was angry on this night. A stiff wind blew still coming out of the northwest as it did earlier in the day. There was a chop on the water and the waves ran two to three feet. Captain Brewster did not raise the sail because the full moon would light it up like a beacon in the night. The white caps sparkled throughout the Sound. Despite the wind whistling through Elijah's hair and the salt spray stinging his face, Elijah was not at all uncomfortable. He found the voyage in the whaleboat pure excitement. The sailors rowed hard, putting their backs into a long pull of the heavy oars. Brewster leaned into the rudder and maintained a straight course for Crane Point at Setauket. Due to the rough sea, Elijah's training with the small swivel cannon was put off for another time. Elijah was disappointed, but he understood. He sat in the bow of the whaleboat right near the swivel gun. At times he would run his hand over it just to experience the feel of the big gun.

At first he didn't know what they were. Popping sounds on the water around the boat. Then one thudded into the side of the whaleboat. They were being fired upon! He turned and saw another boat about thirty or forty yards behind them on the port side. The other boat, much bigger and under sail, was gaining on them. Captain Brewster saw them as well and was issuing orders.

"Munson, take the rudder. Elijah change places with Thorne in the second seat. Quickly, boy, quickly now." Brewster moved forward and grasping the seventeen foot mast and sail as if it were a toy, stepped the mast into position. As the sail unfurled in the strong wind, Brewster returned to the rudder and shouted additional orders.

"Ship oars. Pull on that sheet and tighten that sail."

"Can we outrun them?" shouted Elijah over the wind.

"Sure we can. But we won't," said Brewster.

The larger boat was gaining on them. The musket shots were getting closer. Elijah got a good look at the men in the attacking vessel.

"They're not Redcoats!" said Elijah startled by his own discovery.

"Of course not, boy. It's those damn marauding cowboys. We can outrun them, but I'll never run from the likes of them."

"Cale, shall I deep six the package?"

"Stand steady, my lad. The package is still safe. Prepare to come about, men. Horne, is that gun at the ready?"

"Yes, Captain, I'm ready."

Elijah's heart was pounding with excitement and he felt trepidations and twinges of fear. The men around him appeared calm and matter-of-fact in their actions. Elijah watched as Brewster and his men checked their weapons and realized that he too, had instinctively drawn his pistol as well.

"Prepare to come about," bellowed Brewster, and then after only a moment, "Come about!"

The whaleboat's sail swung from the starboard to the port side as Brewster pulled hard on the tiller. The whaleboat spun around and now with doubled speed the two boats approached each other.

"Now, Thorne, now!" shouted Captain Brewster.

A small explosion ensued as the swivel gun blasted at the larger boat. The cannon shot hit the mast about midway, shattering it and sending wood and canvas down upon the enemy vessel. As the boats passed each other, Caleb Brewster and his men fired upon the occupants of the floundering vessel. Thorne had reloaded the small cannon and as the whaleboat came about once again, he sent a ball into the stern of the enemy boat. Brewster and his men circled the sinking vessel and fired upon them once again. The men on the attacking vessel returned their fire, but with their boat sinking fast, they were no match for Brewster's men. The battle was over very quickly and moments later the sinking vessel with its dead and dying crew, disappeared beneath the water of the Devil's Belt. The whaleboat continued on its way toward Setauket. Without so much as a backward glance Brewster ordered, "Down sail."

The sail and mast were stepped down and soon they were back on course as if nothing had happened. Elijah looked about him in disbelief. His mouth was wide open and he stared at the spot where the boat had been.

"You can put your gun away, boy. They're gone now," said Brewster with a smile. The men laughed and Elijah realized that he had drawn his pistol, but was so amazed at the precision and quickness of Caleb Brewster and his men, that he had not fired once. Elijah put his gun away and thought it best that he say nothing at all.

FOURTEEN

Austin Roe entered the coffee house and sat at a small table by the window. He deliberately chose a window table that would give him a clear view of all the patrons of the establishment. He was visibly exhausted, hungry, and thirsty as well. He had just completed the long hard ride from Setauket and his lanky frame ached from head to toe. A waiting girl approached him and made an attempt to wipe clean the table top. He smelled of sweat, both his and the horse's, and his trousers were soaked with lather from the mare's hard run.

"Would'ja like somethin, sir?" she asked.

"Coffee . . . No, rum. I tell you girl, you'd better bring me both. And bring some mutton, cold or hot, it doesn't matter."

"No mutton t'day, sir. We 'ave beef. Ta yer likin, sir?"

"Okay, bring the beef," said Roe to the girl as she quickly departed, "and some bread, please," he shouted after her.

He removed his three-cornered hat and tossed it on the window ledge. Running his fingers through his thick black hair and then over his face, he tried to rub away the fatigue.

He looked about the rather large room. The coffee shop was busy for this early evening hour. Within another hour it would be bustling with dinner patrons and early evening revelers. The establishment had become favored by the British officers. Each officer endeavored to become friendly with Robert Townsend who, besides his position as a New York merchant and owner of this coffee shop, also wrote articles for the Royal Gazette which slanted the news pro-tory. The officers wanted favorable publicity in the magazine so they cultivated Townsend's friendship. They would rush to Townsend with news of their promotions, changes of operations, and new importance to their own careers. Townsend was cunning enough to glean from them the facts he wanted, information vital to General Washington and the Continental Army.

Robert Townsend had changed his manner and dress to assume the polished appearance and airs of a Tory businessman. He spent hours before a mirror curling his chestnut hair and practicing their foppish attitude. He now looked the part he needed to gain the confidence of the English gentry. He had forced himself to become a social snob.

Austin Roe saw Townsend in deep conversation with three British officers. He could tell from their smiles and their frequent nods of approval that Townsend was promising them the publicity they craved.

Townsend, on occasion, also looked about the room. No sign of recognition passed between them but Austin knew that he had been seen by Townsend. He sat quietly eating and after fifteen or twenty minutes, watched as Robert Townsend excused himself from the British officers. Without so much as a glance in Roe's direction, Townsend left the coffee house.

Roe also remained discreet in his actions. He slowly finished his tankard of rum and flirted with the waiting girl as he paid for his meal. More and more red-coated officers, some with fashionable women on their arm, came into the coffee house. Roe left as quietly as he had entered. He made his way back the same way he had come, passing the stables where a stable boy was brushing down his mare. He entered Townsend & Company through a back door. Robert Townsend was waiting for him in his private quarters above the shop.

"You look tired, Austin."

"I am. Very. Here, a message from Bolton," said Roe as he flopped in a chair and stretched out his long legs.

Townsend opened the letter and laid it flat on his desk. He ignored the writing and sliding back a panel of wood from the wall, opened a small secret closet. He withdrew a phial of liquid and moistened a small piece of cloth. Lightly passing the damp cotton cloth between the written lines of Bolton's letter, he was once again amazed by the magic of the secret stain. He finished reading the message and after committing it to memory, placed it in a metal pan. Using a phosphoric taper he ignited the message and waited as it burned to be sure that every bit of the cryptic message was destroyed. Townsend had purchased the fire starting device specifically for that purpose. Although they were expensive, for Townsend and the Culper Ring, it was cheaper than discovery. Austin found the tapers more intriguing than the invisible ink, but tonight he was too exhausted to observe either.

Townsend took a clean sheet of paper and started to write. He stopped and looked over at Austin Roe. "Sleep if you can, Austin, but only until I finish this message. This information is extremely important and must get to Bolton tonight. I'm sorry, I know how tired you are, but you must go as soon as this is properly coded and prepared. I'll write it using the secret stain on a letter to that British Colonel in Setauket who was just robbed. Everyone knows about the robbery and will expect him to be buying merchandise. He has already ordered from me. I'll just discuss something about his order."

"I'll go if I must, of course, but what about Hawkins? Can't you get him for this ride? I really am dead on my feet."

"I wouldn't ask if there was another way. Jonas Hawkins is ill with the fever. There's only you."

"I'll go, but a little sleep is out of the question. If I may wash, it'll refresh me."

"There's a pitcher of water and a wash basin over on that cabinet. Towels in the first drawer."

"What makes this message so important?" asked Austin as he poured water into the wash basin. He spoke in a hushed tone even though both men were sure that they could not be overheard. He splashed cool water on his face and neck and it seemed to revive him. As he washed himself he looked to Townsend for an answer.

"The French have come to help us. Whether they believe in our cause or just want to aggravate the English is of little importance at this time. Their fleet is landing in Newport, Rhode Island. It seems, the English know about the French and are getting ready to attack them. You know the confusion of foreign ships entering a port for the first time. The French fleet of seven ships will be bottled up. They'll be vulnerable, having no time to erect fortifications. The English, Sir Henry Clinton in charge, are sending eleven ships of the line. The French will be destroyed. Washington must be told so that he can warn our new friends who have come to aid us."

Austin Roe finished washing. "The message will get through, and tonight," said Roe as he dried his face and placed the towel on the Cabinet.

"I'll finish this in just a few minutes."

"What else will I be carrying?"

"Just this letter to that Colonel Floyd and a few other letters. I won't burden you with any unnecessary weight. I don't want to slow down your horse. Oh! Speaking of horses, there's a new gelding in the stable. He, I've been told, is lightning fast and was placed in my care for just such a need."

"Placed in your care? By whom?"

"Sent by General George Washington, himself. He's even paying for the feed and care. Of course, I can prove that I purchased the horse from a farmer in Westchester if the need arises."

"I'll be careful with the general's horse."

"Don't be concerned with the horse. Never has a message been more urgent, and time is of the essence. The British are preparing to move as we speak. They're aware of the importance of surprising the French. I was told that they have tightened security in and out of the city. I'm sure that they will be stopping everyone."

"That I'm sure is true, but they'd expect a message such as this one to be going north out of the city, not south and by way of the Island."

"Be careful, Austin, so much depends on this. You must be alert for anything. Go now. We waste time talking. Go now and may God ride with you."

*

Austin knew that the horse was fast. He had the look of a thoroughbred about him. He also sensed, as he mounted, that the horse was itching for a hard ride. He too, was anxious to see just what the horse could do but he knew that speed on the roads of New York City would attract undo attention. He set a leisurely pace which moved him along but would not give the Redcoats reason the stop him. Still, Austin was worried.

He was just one street away from the Brooklyn ferry and was starting to feel relieved that he had not been stopped. He had not seen any Redcoats, or Lobsterbacks as they were called in Connecticut and parts north of New York, at all. He rounded the corner on the final approach to the ferry and rode into a dozen or so British soldiers. They were checking everyone going on the ferry. A chill ran up his spine. Was this the night he would be discovered? This night of all nights when the message was so important? He thought of wheeling the horse around and running from the area, but he saw several mounted dragoons standing quietly on a side street just waiting for such a need. The uniforms set them apart as Queens Rangers. Their green coats were dressed in blue with chain shoulder straps and black canvas spatterdashes. Their tall leather caps, crested in bearskin, bore a white crescent bearing the name 'Queen's Rangers'.

Fear gripped at the pit of his stomach. "The message will get through, tonight" is what he had said and that is what he must do. With new resolve he slowed his horse to a walk and approached the soldiers.

"Good evening, Gentlemen. Is the ferry working tonight?" said Austin as casually as possible.

"Dismount your horse," said one Redcoat with a surly tone.

"Oh, I know him," said another. "That's Austin Roe. He works for Townsend & Company. He's all right."

"I don't care who you are or who you work for, get off the horse," said the same rude infantryman. His hands reached for Austin to pull him from his horse.

"I'll . . . I'll get off. Don't need any help, thank you."

"Don't need any damn back talk, either," said the soldier. "Where're you going?"

"Home. To Setauket."

"Carrying anything for your boss?"

"Yes, just a few letters. I have to deliver them tomorrow."

"Where are they?"

"In the saddle bag. I'll get them . . . "

"I'll get them," said the soldier as he pushed Roe to the other Redcoats. "Search him. Search him thoroughly, boots, stockings, everything."

The arrogant Redcoat pulled a packet of letters from the saddle-bags and issued more orders. "Take that saddle off and check it, and the blanket. I'll just read these letters."

"Those are personal and business letters from Mr. Townsend. I don't think tha . . . " Austin Roe's words where cut short by a punch in the mouth. He fell in a heap on the ground as the soldier kicked him several times in the stomach. Austin resisted the urge to fight back. He felt the copper-like taste of blood in his mouth and a surge of anger raced through his body along with the thought, "The message will get through, tonight". With some difficulty he got to his feet as the Redcoat began opening and reading the letters. The Redcoat hesitated when he came to the letter addressed to a British Colonel. Roe felt sure that the soldier would not be brazen enough to open an officer's mail. The soldier thought for a minute and then with a knowing look at Austin, opened the Colonel's letter also. Austin's mind began to panic. Would the secret message hold up? Could something other than the disclosing solution bring the message forward? Perhaps the damp night air? Or the tanning solution from the leather of the saddle bag? Or something on the Redcoat's dirty hands?

"Listen to this," said the Redcoat as Austin's heart was pounding. "Remember that Colonel Floyd who was robbed? He's trying to buy some stuff and is having hard luck with that as well. The letter says, "The articles you want cannot be procured. As soon we get them we will send them on to you." The poor Colonel is having a bad time."

The soldiers were satisfied that Austin Roe was not carrying any messages. They threw the letters in his face and turned their attention upon another hapless traveler that night. Roe picked up the letters, glancing quickly at them to be sure that he still had the letter to Colonel Floyd. He adjusted his clothing, and put on his stockings and boots. Saddling his horse and without so much as a glance at the Redcoats, he left the area and went to the ferry. Austin had been called upon many times to stop fights in his tavern in Setauket, but this was the first time he had to suppress such an overwhelming urge to break another man's head.

He was grateful that the balance of the long ride to Setauket was uneventful. The horse was fast. As Townsend had said, 'fast as Lightning'. The horse was untiring and rather than change horse in Hampstead, and explain the swollen lip, cuts, and bruises to another Redcoat, he walked the new horse for about a mile and then proceeded to Setauket to complete his portion of the ring. Each member was told of the importance of the message and to rush with all speed possible.

Caleb Brewster made record time in crossing the Sound. After decoding and transposing, the message was sent via the fastest dragoon to General Washington. Later that week Tallmadge received a special communication from General Washington which spoke of the success of the Culper Ring. Major Tallmadge finished reading the letter to Elijah.

" . . . and by the efforts of you and your Culper people the French fleet was saved."

"But how was the fleet saved? What did General Washington do with the information the Ring provided?" asked Elijah.

"The General mentions that in his letter. Besides alerting the French, he had to stop the British from leaving New York. He hastily wrote messages and rushed them to New York. They were dropped where they could be found by the British. These letters or messages told of an eminent attack by General Washington upon New York. General Washington had no intention of attacking New

York, but his plan worked and the English, fearing that they needed all the soldiers they had, never left to attack the French".

"It's good to know that we're doing some good," said Elijah.

"The life of a spy is a lonely one. As any soldier, a spy must possess bravery and courage, but a spy must also have that intangible something which includes; poise, absolute control of expression of face and body, tact, fearlessness, and discretion. It is the most dangerous of all ventures and the most unsung. Our failure means our death and any success goes un-heralded," said Major Tallmadge as he stared out of the window and thought of his friend Nathan. Would anyone ever know how much he had given? Would he be remembered?

FIFTEEN

Weary and exhausted, Major Tallmadge and his dragoons returned to their encampment. They had been chasing the marauding British war parties sent by General Tryon which had been burning and looting defenseless villages and farms in Westchester and Connecticut. Tallmadge and his dragoons always seemed to arrive too late to prevent the slaughter and destruction.

Benjamin dismounted in the courtyard outside his home. He patted his horse on the neck as Elijah led him away.

"Thank you, Elijah. I'm sure you'll see to it that he's properly taken care of and fed."

"Yes, sir, Major. And if you don't mind my saying so, sir, you should get some rest as well."

"Yes, I intend to, but first I'll clean up and eat. I'm famished. After you tend to the horses, join me for supper."

"Yes, sir, thank you, I'd like that," said Elijah as he walked the horse off to the stable area.

Tallmadge stood quietly in the courtyard. He stretched his arms outward from his sides and yawned. In the stillness of the night an unfamiliar sound from behind him drew his attention. The major whirled around drawing is pistol as he turned. A large shadow began to form from the darkened area of his porch. The shadow moved steadily toward him.

"Friend of foe? Declare yourself!" said Tallmadge, his pistol leveled at the image approaching him.

"Hold on there, Major. I've been shot at enough by the damn British. Don't need you putting any holes in me."

Benjamin lowered his pistol and smiled as he recognized the

voice of Caleb Brewster. The huge shadow came into the light and smiled at him.

"Damn you, Cale! I could have killed you!"

"You must be tired. I've never known you to curse. You being the son of a minister and all that."

"I'm sorry, Cale and yes, I am tired. I'm both tired and frustrated. I've chased the British for weeks now. I long for a battle, any engagement with the enemy. We've come close so many times to catching these cowards who attack the helpless. But, enough of that, come inside and have some supper with me. Elijah will join us shortly."

"I've eaten, but I'll have a little wine and maybe I can eat a little."

"A little wine? Eat a little? Cale, you never do anything little. Come inside. I'm so hungry, tonight I may eat more than you."

The two men laughed as they entered the house. Tallmadge excused himself and saw to the ordering of food and drink. After washing he returned to the main room. The two comrades-in-arms sat and talked.

"Before I forget, here are the letters from the Culpers, and I've news from Setauket. But first, did I hear you correctly? You haven't caught any of those blasted Lobster-backs?"

"No, we haven't. They have eluded us again. They sacked Tarrytown and Dobbs Ferry and left Danbury and Ridgefield burning. We never know where they'll hit. It seems that they follow no set plan at all."

"Well, unhappily I tell you that they attacked Fairfield today. The town was totally defenseless. Why do they choose to pillage small villages which have no strategic significance for the British?"

"They want to frighten the patriots and possibly prevent collaboration in the transmission of messages across the sound."

"They know about the Culpers?"

"No. But they know that there's information leaking out somewhere and they're trying everything and anything to stop it. We've a problem too. How did the British know that the French fleet was coming? How did the British know when and where they would land and with how many men and ships?"

"Do you suspect one of the Culpers? Those that I know would die before giving information to the British."

"It's not any of the Culpers. General Washington and I have started an investigation. We're asking all those who knew, if they passed the information on, and to whom. It's not any of the Culpers, because when we learned about the French coming, the British already knew. And remember, it was the Culpers who warned General Washington that the French would be attacked."

"Then who knew?"

"After General Washington was told directly by the Marquis de Lafayette that the French were coming, he told some of his generals; General Scott, General Arnold, and a few others. Assuming that the generals are above reproach, we're checking as to whom the generals gave that information."

Caleb Brewster got up and answered a knock at the door. The food had arrived along with Elijah Churchill.

"Hello, Cale . . . er, . . . Captain Brewster," said Elijah.

"Will you stop calling me Captain or do you want me to act like an officer and start ordering you around?"

"All right, Cale. Major Tallmadge, I . . . " Elijah stopped as both men were laughing.

"I'm sorry , sir, but I just couldn't call you, . . . er, by your given name. I . . . you'll always be Major Tallmadge to me, sir. And I mean no disrespect to you, sir . . . er . . . Captain, . . . Cale! This may get confusing. Here, Major, I stopped at regiment headquarters. You have some letters."

"Thank you, Elijah. Put them on my desk. I'll go through them after we eat, but first I had better open this Culper message."

Major Tallmadge opened the Culper message and applied the special revealing liquid. He walked over to where Elijah and Cale was sitting.

"Culper Jr. has a postscript. It seems that the British have placed increased pressure on their efforts to stop information from getting into our hands. Culper Jr. is going to take a short holiday of one week. He suggests that we suspend all Culper operations for that period of time. Perhaps that will be a good idea. He's coming to Oyster Bay to visit his family and will be carrying information with him. Looks like you'll get another trip to Oyster Bay. Would you like that, Elijah?"

Elijah felt himself blush bright red and looked quizzically at Caleb who mimicked a young girl by placing his napkin on top of his head and batting his eyelashes. The three laughed and dove into the food. It was the first meal of the day for Benjamin and Elijah. Caleb had lost count.

They ate in silence for a while, each savoring every morsel. It was Tallmadge who first stopped eating and spoke. "Cale, you mentioned that you have news from Setauket. What news?"

"Ben, you're not going to like it. Your father's Presbyterian church has been taken over as barracks for the British. They've desecrated the cemetery and fortified the church with the tombstones. They also smashed the stain glass windows to stick their damn guns through. I took five hundred men and attempted to dislodge the British. Would've done it too, but a British Man-O-War showed up in Setauket harbor. After fighting for hours we had to leave. We got away with their horses and most of their military supplies. They're hurting, but we didn't destroy them as we wanted to."

"And what of my father?"

"He wanted to stay on the farm, but I talked him into going into hiding. He's on Strong's Neck with Anna and her sister. He's in good hands."

"Thank you for caring for him, Cale. For safety's sake I think he should come here."

"I wanted to bring him, but ... "

"On the next trip, bring him back with you even if you have to bind and gag him."

"I will, but I think he wants to stay, well because ... Benjamin, you know how lonely your father has been since your mother passed away. I think your father, . . . well he sort of likes Anna's sister, Zipporah."

"Well then, bring them both," said Tallmadge as he thumbed through the letters that Elijah had brought. One letter caught his eye. It was from General Benedict Arnold. He read it quickly and then reread it. Looking up from the letter he asked, "Has either of you ever heard of a man called John Anderson?"

"No, sir, not I."

"Nor I," said Cale. "Who is he?"

"I don't know, but if he ever shows up here, General Arnold has requested that I give him safe conduct with a protective guard of dragoons, and send him to General Arnold after first sending an express rider telling the general that he's coming. This is strange. Elijah, see that this is seen by all the officers so that they are also aware of, what's his name? Oh, here it is, Anderson, John Anderson. Also, tomorrow you'll retrieve the messages from Culper Jr. in Oyster Bay. Cale, I'd like you to take him and on the way back slip into Setauket and get my father and whoever else he may want to bring with him."

*

Sally Townsend looked lovelier than ever. As Elijah made his way along the road to her home he could see her in the gardens gathering flowers for her mother. The weather was warm for September and she was wearing a simple white linen summer dress with ruffled cuffs. She wore a wide brim straw hat with a rather large white ribbon on it. Her black hair and sparkling blue eyes were matched only by her radiant smile and her flawless complexion.

Elijah watched her from the white picket fence by the garden as she went about picking flowers. She was in a very happy mood and hummed a little song as she gathered her bouquet. She saw him standing there and looked away. After a moment she looked back. It had been some time since she had seen Elijah and he had indeed changed.

"Elijah? Elijah, is that really you?"

"Yes, Sally, but shouldn't you call me James?"

"Oh, Poo! There's no one here, and they wouldn't remember even if they were."

"No one here? I must see your brother, Robert," said Elijah as he jumped over the low picket fence.

"Oh, he's here. I mean that the soldiers aren't here. At least they aren't here now. What are you staring at?"

"You. Just you. You're more beautiful than I remembered."

"So you didn't remember me?"

"Yes, but I didn't remem ... er ... Could you tell your brother that I'm here?"

"Certainly. Come and sit in the gazebo and I'll get him."

"No need, Sarah," called Robert Townsend from an upstairs window. "I'll be down directly."

"Am I only to see you once a year?" asked Sally.

"If only I could see you more often."

"Why don't you? What's stopping you? The next time you see me I might be married, or engaged to be. Forgive me. I'm told I'm too impetuous."

"Are you seeing someone?"

"What does that mean?" said Sally flashing hers eyes over the top of the bouquet.

"You know what I mean."

"Well I see lots of people. If you mean men friends, well, I see them too. So many young good-looking soldiers that it could turn a girl's head."

"Soldiers! Do you mean the Redcoats?"

"Some of them are handsome and they're all interested in me. Why even Colonel Simcoe sent me a Valentine. Let me get it. I'll show it to you."

"No! Thank you, Sally. I'm not interested in seeing any Valentine!" said Elijah both embarrassed and angry.

Robert Townsend appeared with two glasses of lemon refreshers. He set the glasses down on the steps near the gazebo. The tinkling ice sparkled in the sunlight. As refreshing as they looked Elijah said, "Thank you, sir, but I'm not thirsty. If we could but do our business then . . . "

"At least wipe your sweaty brow with the napkin."

"Sir?"

"The napkin, Elijah," said Robert as he returned to the house.

Elijah picked up the napkin and could feel the added thickness of the messages. Taking the messages, he laid the napkin beside the glass.

"Thank your brother for me for the lemon refresher and good day to you, Miss Sally." He once again leaped over the picket fence and still propelled by anger, stormed down the road in the direction of the bay and the waiting whaleboat.

Sally watched him go. He had changed, for the better. Less of a boy, so much more a man. Her eyes followed him down the road. She hoped that he would turn around but he didn't. She thought to herself, "Sally Townsend, what has your foolishness done?"

*

Before the week was up, Elijah had to return to the Townsend home to bring messages to Culper Jr. Elijah dreaded meeting with Sally once again and yet he also looked forward to seeing her. Although only less than a week had passed, the weather had changed. The evening was chilly as he approached the Townsend house. He checked the grounds about the house, but there were no Redcoats about on this particular evening. Elijah went directly to the back door and knocked. He hoped that Sally would answer but it was her father, the senior Townsend, who came to the door.

"Yes, young man, what can I do for you?" said Samuel Townsend.

"Good evening, sir. I'm here to see Sally, if I may?"

"Who is it, Father?" said Sally's sister, Phoebe.

"Have him wait in the gazebo," called Sally from an upstairs room.

"That'll be fine sir. I'll wait in the gazebo," said Elijah. He turned and walked into the gardens. He did not want to get involved with introductions and the like, especially when he knew that British officers were living there. He felt for the packet of messages in his pocket. How would he pass it to Robert Townsend. He pondered over what to do. Dare he give them to Sally? No, he couldn't involve her.

The garden gate swung open. He could hear voices of men in conversation. He watched as two officers walked into the gardens from the gate by the front of the house. The heavy-set man was a Lieutenant Colonel. He had to be Simcoe, the Valentine sender. The other officer was tall and handsome, a major in an elegant uniform. Elijah didn't know who he was but a pang of jealousy gripped him.

Other Redcoats were gathering in the garden. What if he ran into the same group as he did before? He could not allow a search. It would endanger the entire Townsend family and the Culper Ring. The back door opened and Robert Townsend emerged. He obviously was going to Elijah at the gazebo, but when he ran into the officers he greeted them and returned to the house with them. He never once looked toward the gazebo.

Elijah leaned further back on the bench into the shadows of the gazebo. His hand hit a flower pot and almost knocked it over. He caught it just in time. He returned it in its place with the other five flower pots. Six pots, just like the six handkerchiefs on Anna Strong's clothes line. Robert Townsend had to know. Elijah glanced about the gardens. It was now or never. He quickly placed the packet of messages under the second pot. Satisfied that it would go unnoticed, he sat back and waited for Sally.

He didn't have long to wait. Sally came running from the other side of the house toward the gazebo. She saw him and hastened to sit by his side. Her smile was like a bouquet of fresh flowers and

Elijah could not help but smile back at her. His heart was pounding and he felt a funny feeling on the back of his neck as she said his name and took his hand.

"Elijah. I'm so glad that you are not angry with me. You aren't are you?"

"No, I'm not angry with you. I was but … not now … Not any more."

"I acted foolishly. Do you have something for my brother? Give it to me. He cannot possibly see you. Colonel Simcoe and Major Andre have just arrived."

"I won't endanger you. Just tell your brother to remember who I am, where I was sitting and to think of handkerchief number two. I hope he knows what I'm talking about. If not, he's intelligent enough to figure it out. God help me if he isn't."

"I'd like you to stay with me, but this place will be swarming with officers within the hour. They're having some sort of a meeting and my brother has offered the use of our home."

"You're right. It's best that I leave. If I go that way over the back fence I have a chance of not being seen."

"Right now that is the only way you can go."

"Good-bye, Sally. For now."

"Good-bye, Elijah. I hope that someday we'll see each other again."

The space between them closed as they looked deeply into each other's eyes. Elijah closed his eyes tightly. He could feel Sally move even closer to him. He opened his eyes when he felt their bodies touch. They kissed quickly and Elijah left the gazebo, slipped silently into the dark shadows, and disappeared into the night. Suddenly Sally felt a chill. She brushed a tear away and walked slowly back to the house.

SIXTEEN

Sally sat alone in the gazebo clutching a small shawl about her against the coolness of the evening. Two days had passed since she had watched Elijah disappear into the night. The night was clear and the full moon cast a pale glow on the house. She thought how remarkable it was that she could see so well at this time of night. She was deep in thought when she heard the creak of the gate by the side of the house. She watched silently from the shadows of the gazebo to see who it was who would come through that seldom used entrance. A short stocky man appeared and walked softly around the house. Sally recognized him as a neighbor who lived in the town about three streets away. She was about to call out to him when she noticed that his actions appeared strange. He kept looking cautiously about the grounds and into the windows. Sally knew that she could not be seen in the gazebo and yet she remained as still as she could, trying to even hold her breath.

No one was at home so she felt there was no need to warn anyone. The cautious neighbor went to the back door and stepped into the house. Putting her fears behind her, Sally ran to the window to see what the man was doing. She could see him enter the small room off the kitchen. Moving to that window and keeping to the side so that she would not be seen, Sally watched the obviously nervous man approach a cupboard which the family seldom used. He opened a drawer and slipped a folded sheet of paper into it.

His task completed, the man hastened to leave the house. Sally ran and hid behind the lilac bushes so she would not be discovered. She watched the man leave the house and then waited until she once again heard the creak of the side gate announce his departure.

After a moment Sally went to the cupboard and took the letter. It appeared to be a business letter addressed to a John Anderson and it mentioned the American Army facilities at West Point. Of what interest would a businessman have with West Point? She replaced the letter and that evening never strayed too far from the kitchen area so that she could see who would eventually come for the letter. She didn't have to wait too long. Shortly after dinner she watched as Major Andre secreted a tray of her freshly baked doughnuts into the small room by the kitchen. Later, when the doughnuts could not be found, he disappeared into the little room and returned with the doughnuts saying he had hid them just to tease the girls.

Sally went to the cupboard and found that the letter had been taken. Major Andre was the only person who could have taken the letter. Why would Major Andre take a letter addressed to John Anderson? Suddenly, the letter which mentioned West Point, had new meaning since it had been taken by a British officer.

Sally was in a turmoil over this situation. Should she tell her brother Robert? If only he had stayed another day. She went to her room to think and decide what to do. Passing Colonel Simcoe's room she heard him in conversation with Major Andre. The words were muffled and unclear but one thing was certain. They were talking about West Point, of that she was sure. It was now also very clear that Robert must be told.

Sally was perplexed. She couldn't tell anyone else of her findings, and she didn't know how to get the information to her brother, although she knew that she must. She didn't know whom she could trust. How was she going to get the information to Robert? Only the British could get through to New York without being stopped. Some how she had to use the British. She thought of a long time friend of the family and knowing that he was enamored of her, she sent for him requesting a favor. In less than an hour Captain Daniel Youngs was standing in the hallway of the Townsend home, hat in hand and ready to do the bidding of Sally Townsend.

"Thank you for coming so quickly, Daniel," said Sally using her coy ways and acting shy she partially hid her face behind a letter which she twirled on her fingers.

"Oh, anything for you, Miss Sally. How can I help you?" said the young officer. He could hardly stand still he was so nervous just being near the lovely Miss Sally.

"Daniel, we're having a party tomorrow night and we're completely out of the special tea that so many of the officers enjoy. My family would hate to disappoint them. My brother has the tea in his store in New York. That's the only place it can be gotten. We must have it. Could you send a rider to Robert's store in New York? I'd be forever grateful."

"I don't know, Miss Sally. It is late and . . . "

"I'm sure you would just love this tea, Daniel and I want you to have a special invitation to the party. You'd be my special guest."

"Well, Miss Sally, I really . . . "

"It's Colonel Simcoe's favorite tea. I'd hate to disappoint him. He would feel terrible if he knew that you could've gotten it for him."

"Yes, Miss Sally. I'll do it, but I'll only do it for you."

"Thank you, Daniel. Give this letter to my brother. It'll explain the kind of tea I want. Now you be on your way now. He must have this letter tonight so that he can send the tea back as quickly as possible. Thank you, Daniel, and I'll see you at the party."

"Thank you, Miss Sally and good night. I look forward to the party."

"You'll just love the tea," said Sally as she winked at the blushing Captain.

*

Sally's message had gone full circle and was in Setauket the following morning. It crossed the Sound and Major Tallmadge had it by noon that day. With the revelations of the goings on in

Oyster Bay, new questions arose and new meaning was given to the letter Tallmadge had received from General Benedict Arnold.

Why did General Arnold want to give safe conduct to this John Anderson and what did it all mean in relation to West Point?

While Tallmadge pondered over this latest espionage finding, he and the dragoons were searching for British war parties in the area south of North Castle. That same evening he returned to discover that a man called John Anderson had been captured and turned over to the Second Regiment of Dragoons stationed in North Castle. Lieutenant

Colonel John Jameson was the temporary commanding officer. Anderson had been found with secret papers and diagrams of the military installations of West Point. These papers had been hidden in his boots, which were the actual cause of his capture. The men who seized him did so only to rob him of his boots. When they removed his boots and found the papers, they turned him over to the army hoping to get a reward. Major Tallmadge went immediately to regiment headquarters to speak to Colonel Jameson. Elijah went with him.

"Colonel, I understand that we have a John Anderson in custody. I'd like to interrogate him."

"Good evening, Major. Yes, we did have a Mr. Anderson, but I sent him on to General Arnold."

"You did what?!"

"He had a pass. And, may I remind you of a letter from General Arnold requesting safe conduct for John Anderson. I was just following orders from a superior officer. What else would you suggest I do?"

"He was captured as a spy. You should have waited!"

"I don't like your tone, Major. May I also remind you that I'm your superior officer, a fact you appear eager to forget."

"And you know me well enough to know that I'd not speak this way without good reason." Elijah had never seen the major so angry and agitated.

"And what are those reasons?"

"In these matters I answer only to General Washington. We are wasting time. Recall your order. I'll send my fastest dragoon to catch the spy and his safe conduct party."

"You don't know that he's a spy."

"Damn you, Jameson! Elijah! Take a fresh horse and go after the group that left here . . . how long ago? Jameson! How long ago?"

"Ten, maybe fifteen minutes."

"Go, Elijah, go, and ride like you never rode before."

"If you are wrong, Tallmadge, I'll see that you hang for your impertinence," said the Colonel.

"I'll take that chance. Where are the papers he was carrying?"

"I sent them on . . . to General Washington."

"Well good. At least you didn't send them to Arnold. Now I think we should take an armed guard and hold General Arnold until General Washington can review . . . "

"You're out of your mind. I'll do nothing of the sort. And besides, before I sent Anderson to General Arnold, I notified the General by swift courier that Anderson was being sent as per his request . . . "

"And I suppose the circumstances of his capture?"

"Of course."

"You fool, you damn fool."

*

Elijah went to the stables and sought out the fastest horse available. He saddled him quickly and within minutes of his major's orders, was on the road after the two dragoons and the questionable Mr. Anderson. Elijah knew that the two dragoons would not be traveling quickly. They were in no particular hurry and were basically an escort for Anderson. The horse, a dappled gray, knew what was expected of him and flew over the road toward West Point. The large animal had an effortless gait which ate up the miles of moonlit roads. Elijah never grew tired of the rhythmic sound of the horse's hooves pounding the earth. He loved to ride and felt that it was the closest thing to flying that he could do. In a little less than an hour, Elijah caught sight of three horsemen in the dark shadows on the road ahead of him. The gray horse sped onward closing the gap between Elijah and the three.

"Hold," Elijah shouted ahead to them. The two dragoons drew their weapons thinking Elijah was a highwayman. One of the dragoons took aim with his pistol and was about to fire when he recognized the familiar uniform of a fellow dragoon. Both men quickly sheathed their weapons when they saw it was Sergeant Churchill who was rapidly approaching them.

Elijah's horse reared to a stop and kept prancing and pawing at the ground, as if emphasizing the urgency of his rider's mission.

"Major Tallmadge has returned and he's ordered the recall of this man," said Elijah as he pointed in the direction of John Anderson who sat silently on his horse. Elijah looked at Anderson, but couldn't see his face since he was wearing a cloak with a large hood.

"But our orders come from Colonel Jameson," said the corporal.

"Colonel Jameson was with Major Tallmadge when I was ordered to recall Mr. Anderson and his guard to headquarters at North Castle. I didn't question my orders.

Why should you? We're returning to North Castle now."

The four men turned their horses and headed back. Elijah wondered why this man had caused Major Tallmadge to become so upset. Who was he and why the mystery about him. Elijah looked again at Anderson, but his face was still bathed in shadows.

*

Benjamin Tallmadge paced the floor, impatiently waiting for the return of John Anderson, Elijah, and the dragoons. He prayed that Elijah would be able to catch Anderson and the escort. Benjamin had gone to his quarters on the post and washed himself after the long tiring day. Although he had the time, he refused food as he was too aggravated to eat. He returned to headquarters and waited with Colonel Jameson. The hours passed slowly and Benjamin became more irritable.

He rushed to the windows when he heard the sound of the returning dragoons and looked out toward the stable area. A tall slim man in plain common clothes, dismounted his horse. Benjamin's eyes caught the gleam of the high polish of fine black leather boots. The boots did not fit the clothing. This man must be John Anderson. Tallmadge watched as Anderson and the three dragoons approached. Anderson's walk and carriage was that of a gentleman. Benjamin thought, "This man didn't belong in the clothes he was wearing."

Major Tallmadge greeted his men, ordered two to stand guard and Elijah to bring in the prisoner. Elijah brought Anderson into the room, saluted his major, and stepped back at attention awaiting further orders. Tallmadge turned his full attention on Anderson.

"You are John Anderson?" asked Tallmadge.

"Yes, I'm Anderson. Why has my journey to West Point been interrupted once again? Why am I being held prisoner?"

"You were carrying information regarding the military installations of West Point. You're not in uniform although you appear to be born to the military."

"I was taking that information to West Point under orders from General Benedict Arnold. Must my wrists be bound? I am most uncomfortable!"

"Elijah, untie this gentleman. I presume you are a gentleman and do not usually wear the garments you are presently wearing. But, back to the point of your detention. Why were you carrying the information in your boot?"

"I was protecting it from such sluggards as did set upon me on the road to West Point."

"Why would you bring this particular information to West Point? Certainly West Point has no need of it."

John Anderson avoided the question and raised his bound wrists to Elijah so that they could more readily be untied. Once Anderson was untied he rubbed his wrists and removed the hood from his head. In doing so, Elijah was able to see his face. He stepped back, behind and away from the prisoner.

"Major Tallmadge, sir! Forgive the interruption, but I must speak with you, sir."

"Yes, Elijah? Go ahead, you may speak."

"I'm sorry, sir. May we speak outside, sir?"

The major knew that Elijah wouldn't interrupt if he didn't have a good reason. He nodded to Elijah and followed him outside.

"What's this all about?"

"First, sir, I suggest that you send in the guards to watch the prisoner very carefully."

Tallmadge turned and gave orders to the guards. Then turning back to Elijah he tilted his head in a curious, impatient, and an inquisitive manner.

"This man isn't who he says he is. I couldn't tell you inside, but I saw him in Oyster Bay at the Townsend home. He's a close friend of Colonel Simcoe. He was in uniform when I last saw him. A British uniform. This man is Major John Andre!"

"Elijah, are you sure?"

"Yes, sir, I am. That man who calls himself Anderson is a spy."

"And that especially sickens me, for now I know for sure that General Benedict Arnold is a traitor. Thank you, Elijah, for your keen observation."

Major Tallmadge continued the interrogation and finally without any pressure on his part, the prisoner admitted to being Major John Andre, adjutant to a general of the British Army. He admitted crossing the lines to obtain information. Later, he wrote a letter to General Washington requesting that nothing dishonorable happen to him as he was only serving his King.

Three days later Major Tallmadge was traveling with the dragoons back to his home base. As they rode together, Elijah spoke about things that were bothering him.

"What'll happen to Major Andre? I know he's safely in the stockade and under constant guard, but what'll happen to him eventually?"

"He'll be held for trail. With the evidence against him, I'm sure he'll hang as a spy. My friend, Nathan did, and without the trail."

"There are rumors about the camp that General Arnold was a traitor working with Major Andre."

"Not just rumor. It's a fact. Benedict Arnold conspired with the British to turn West Point over to them. He was probably the one who told the British about the French fleet at Newport."

"Why, sir? General Arnold was an American hero a great patriot. He distinguished himself in so many battles. He was severely wounded in his left leg at the battle of Saratoga and still he fought on . . . "

"Yes, yes, I know the story, although badly wounded his courage led his men to victory. But that was then. I don't know why he changed, but it almost cost us West Point. You know, if it wasn't for the Culpers, who uncovered this plot, the traitor would've succeeded and who knows what direction the war would have taken?"

"What will happen to him, . . . to General Arnold?"

"Will you please stop referring to that traitor as General. He no longer deserves the honor. You ask what will happen to him? Well, as you know he did escape to the British lines, probably thanks to that courier sent by Jameson. Since he couldn't give the British West Point, they'll not welcome him with open arms. He'll serve them in some capacity, but mark my words, the English don't like traitors any more than we do. They'll not trust him and I doubt that any will serve under him."

"What'll happen to him if General Washington captures him?"

"I know what I would do. I'd cut off the leg that was wounded at Saratoga and bury it with full military honors. Then I'd hang the rest of him. Even that would be too good for him."

SEVENTEEN

The carts moved slowly through the narrow streets of New York. Their large wooden wheels made crunching sounds as they slipped and slid between the cobblestones. The cries of the men and women who were packed into the carts and wagons brought crowds of spectators even at this early morning hour. Those in the carts and wagons, some still in their bed clothes, were bound to the sides or to each other. They appeared to come from all walks of life but their cries of pain and woe were the same. Some had been beaten and were still unconscious, lying on the bottom of the carts. Redcoats were marching single file on either side of the unhappy parade. A single drum beat out a slow rhythmic cadence. The spectators were quiet, for anyone who showed too much concern for those in the wagons was taken, bound, and thrown in with them. The mules labored up and down the hilly cobblestone roads spurred onward by their drivers and the whips. The Redcoats shouted curses at the prisoners and the crowd alike. The crowd was stilled as sometimes a Redcoat would take the whip from the mule driver and use it on the prisoners. As the carts and wagons passed the establishments of Townsend & Company, an axle on one gave way under the weight of the wagon. The wagon crashed to the ground and the wheel rolled into the crowd sending them running and screaming. The procession was stopped, the wagon was emptied of its prisoners, and repairs were started by the soldiers who continually cursed the wagon, the prisoners, and the crowd. Robert Townsend heard the commotion and stepped into the street.

"What is happening?" he asked a stranger.

"The British have captured all these people. They're being

taken to the prison ships," said the stranger. He had a surly look about him and he gazed at Robert's frills and velvet with disdain.

"What have they done? What are the charges against them?"

"Don't know," he answered while spitting into the road, just missing Robert.

Robert pushed his way through the growing crowd to get a closer look. He approached a guard and in his quiet way again asked the same questions.

"They're spies. All spies, every one of 'em," said the soldier. "Step back now, away from the prisoners."

Robert pushed rapidly through the crowds by the road, his eyes searching the wagons and carts for any familiar face. Hoping he would see no one that he knew, he crossed between wagons over to the other side and resumed his search, face by face, wagon by wagon. He was almost to the end of the long line of carts. He was becoming more and more relieved that none of his 'assistants' had been captured. He crossed the road once again and was making his way back when, there in the second cart, he saw her.

A gasp escaped him and he coughed to cover the sound which had caused a guard to turn toward him. She had seen him also and as she stared at him, her eyes wild with fear, she slowly shook her head as a signal that he should do nothing in her behalf.

Robert resisted his first instinct to go to her and take her from the wagon. Although his body was immobile his mind raced with thoughts and questions as to what action to take. He was bewildered and frightened. All he could do was stare at the woman who had become so much a part of his life. Her auburn hair was disheveled as were her clothes. Her cheek was bruised and at the corner of her mouth was a small trickle of blood. One of the guards must have hit her. Anger welled up within him and he wanted to strike the guard nearest her.

Robert took a step toward her. Her eyes flashed fear for him and again she shook her head. No, do nothing. He couldn't help her. His head and chest were pounding. He became dizzy and feared he may pass out. Sweating profusely, a wave of nausea passed through him. To prevent himself from crying out he placed his hand firmly over his mouth. It helped hide a face distorted by fear and anguish. They both had known that either or both of them could be captured. Robert thought of the other night at a quiet secretive dinner in a hidden back room when they had spoken of that possibility.

*

"I cannot let you continue. The danger is too great," said Robert.

"I understand your concern, but you cannot stop me. The work you do is important and I have given you valuable information."

"Yes, my love, but if you were caught, I couldn't help you. Even General Washington couldn't help. He and the Culpers don't even know your name. I gave you a code number. Number 355. If the British were . . . "

"Oh, Robert, we so seldom are able to be together, must we talk about the British and the war?"

"You're right, my love," said Robert taking her hand. "Let's talk about the happiness we'll have forever, once the war is over."

"Yes, Robert, once the war is over."

*

His eyes clouded over, but he suppressed the tears as the reality of her imprisonment shook him. As the wagons started up again, she could no longer control her tears as she looked upon the face of the man she loved. She watched him as the wagon moved away, then squaring her shoulders, Culper agent 355 faced the front of the wagon and her uncertain future. With her head held high and proud and the morning sun dancing on the fire-red glow of her hair, Robert watched her as she disappeared from view. He became aware of his tears as he turned and slowly walked away.

Once in the coffee house, he gulped down a large cup of coffee and began to think of how he could help his lady. He felt that he could not continue as Culper Jr., but he would never quit as long as he was of any help for the American cause. He though of sending an urgent coded message about the capture of agent 355, but it would be of no avail. The Culpers could not help. He would notify the Ring of the capture of one of its agents with the next regular courier. The door opened and a middle-aged British officer of his acquaintance entered the coffee house.

"Good morning, Mr. Townsend."

"Good morning, Colonel," said Robert trying to compose himself.

"We had a great morning's work. Rounded up quite a few."

"Is that what was all that commotion this morning? And what was it that you rounded up a few of?"

"Spies. Must've caught a hundred or so."

"That many? Are you sure that they're all spies?"

"Oh, we're sure, and so what if they aren't. If they aren't spies then undoubtedly they must know a spy."

"Surely they could gain their freedom if they'd name other spies."

"You know, we offered just that arrangement, but all claim innocence of any knowledge of spies. We wouldn't let'em go even if they named all the spies."

"I though I recognized one them in one of the wagons."

"Oh, Mr. Townsend, it wouldn't be a good idea to mention that to anyone. General Clinton is in a rage over the hanging of Major Andre and the whole Arnold-West Point affair. He's determined to destroy the American spy ring at all cost. Even though you're a friend of the British, a loyalist, he'd throw you in prison with the rest."

"Where will the prisoners be held for trail?"

"Trial? Ha! Ha! They'll get no trial. This bunch'll go directly to the prison ship, probably the *Jersey*."

Robert Townsend could feel his stomach turn as he forced a smile for the benefit of the officer.

*

In among the following messages from Culper Jr. was information of the general round-up of many suspected spies in New York. Tallmadge was informed that to Culper Jr.'s knowledge, all but one were just American sympathizers. The one was agent 355, a Culper spy. Major Tallmadge knew nothing of this spy other than the code number. He didn't know that the spy was a woman or how much the woman meant to Robert Townsend. He was assured by Townsend that the spy ring was intact and that agent 355 would die before disclosing the name of Culper Jr., who was the agent's only contact with the ring.

Major Tallmadge never knew that it took Robert Townsend longer to write that message than any other message he had ever sent by way of the Culper Ring.

EIGHTEEN

Major Tallmadge greeted two of his dragoon officers, Elijah, Captain Brewster, and two of Brewster's trusted men, Davis and Smith, and welcomed them into his home.

"Come, come in," said Tallmadge. The dragoons saluted smartly. Brewster's men fumbled an attempt at a salute, and Brewster himself, just winked at Tallmadge. The major smiled through all this and waited until they had seated themselves. The dragoons, of course, remained at attention and had to be told to be at their ease and seat themselves.

"Gentlemen, I have this day received orders from General Washington to attack the forts on Long Island. He somehow received information regarding the increased buildup in grain and other dry goods as well as troops and munitions." Elijah smiled at the mention of information and Benjamin returned the knowledgeable wink to Cale. "The general has looked with favor upon my suggestion to destroy the forts, St. George and Slongo. We start with Fort St. George. I've made some plans. Captain Brewster, we'll need your whaleboats to take us across the Sound. The element of surprise is ours and we'll use it."

"When do we start?" asked the jovial giant, his eyes flashing with the excitement of the impending battle.

"It'll take a few hours to finalize our plans and for the preparations. We leave tonight and will attack Fort St. George by noon tomorrow."

Elijah was also excited about the impending battles. He hadn't really been in battle since Trenton and then hardly at all.

*

The early evening was exceptionally cold for November and the heavy clouds threatened rain. Tallmadge and Elijah were the last to board Brewster's whaleboat. Brewster had supervised the entire operation and it was his boat which finally pulled away from the Connecticut shore and took position at the head of the small armada. Their sails billowed outward catching the offshore breeze. The dull drab gray colors of the sailcloth blended with the sky, the fog, and the water. Elijah moved to the stern of the boat and sat with Caleb. The small invasion had begun.

"Do you think it'll rain, Cale?" asked Elijah.

"Rain? Not just rain, boy, we're in for a storm."

"How can you tell?"

"When you've spent as much time as I have at sea, you don't have to 'tell'. I feel it, boy. I feel it. We'll have a storm by morning."

The waters were choppy and the wind increased. The weather was indeed getting quite inclement. The clouds darkened from gray to black and a slight drizzle began to fall.

"One good thing about this weather, Cale," said Tallmadge as he called out from the bow of the boat. "The British can't see us coming."

"That's true, but if anymore of your dragoons get seasick, they'll smell us coming."

"Most of these men have never been at sea and —"

"Just joking, Ben, just joking, and they'll be fine once they get their feet back on solid land."

The small fleet carrying sixty men and officers seemed a puny force to send against the might of England. The men, forty dragoons and twenty of Brewster's men, knew that their cause was right and the thought of defeat was not considered. The crossing of the Devil's Belt was uneventful. The men were quiet with the exception of the few seasick souls who retched their way across. The sight of the shoreline lifted their spirits but no cheer was raised, for fear of raising the British as well. The whaleboats were pulled onto the beaches and hidden in the tall grasses. As the men began to make their way inland, true to Caleb's prediction, a fierce storm came upon them.

The sky lit up with flashes of lightning. Crooked fingers of light opened the heavens and scraped the ground with clawed finger tips. Thunder rolled from cloud to earth and rumbled among the small war-party of patriots. They continued their march inland until a bolt of lightning crashed to earth splitting a large oak tree directly in their path. The tree blazed for a moment or two before a downpour of rain smothered it. The smell of burnt wood hung in the air. All the men stood where they were and waited for orders. Major Tallmadge ran to Brewster as he began to bark orders to his men. The rain continued. The wind roared and lashed out at the men who quickly protected their muskets and gunpowder.

"Cale," shouted Tallmadge over the roar of the storm. "How long will this last?"

"Can't be sure, Ben, but at least most of the morning."

"We must find shelter or we'll be in no condition to fight."

"Our best shelter will be the whaleboats."

"I'm sorry, Cale, couldn't hear you . . . the thunder. What'd you say?"

Caleb Brewster waited until the last peal of thunder rolled away and then repeated himself. "We should go back to the whaleboats. We'll turn them over and get under them. They'll protect us from the storm."

Major Tallmadge nodded and turned to Elijah. "Elijah, tell Captain Edgar and Lieutenant Kanfert that we're going back to the boats. We'll use them as protection from the storm."

"Tell them to get under the same boats they arrived in. Will you do that, boy?" said Brewster.

"Yes, sir, Major and yes, I will, Cale."

*

The storm raged for hours as the gallant invaders huddled unceremoniously under the whaleboats. They seldom spoke as the sound of their voices were magnified by the hollow in which they hid. The storm and its extended duration caused Major Tallmadge to change his plans.

"Elijah, pass the word to the men to get as much sleep as they can. We'll leave at nightfall, march across the island and attack tomorrow morning before sunrise. Also get word to Lieutenant Kanfert to rotate the guards."

Elijah lifted the sail, which was now both door and storm protection for the occupants of the whaleboat, and stepped out into a heavy rain. The lightning and thunder had subsided, but the wind and rain continued unabated. The wind at times was so violent that trees lashed out at the sky threatening to be ripped from the earth that held them.

Because of the wind the rain moved at times horizontally and occasionally even upward. Elijah sloshed through puddles of sand and mud as he went from whaleboat to whaleboat. Sometimes the wind stopped his forward movement and he would push against it as if it were a wall. He finally returned to his whaleboat with a new appreciation for its protection. There he slept with the rest of the men until the storm was over.

The men greeted the end of the storm and the oncoming darkness with elation. They stretched and yawned after hours of sleep in extremely cramped quarters. Within the hour, as darkness gathered about them, Major Tallmadge had his troop of hand-picked men on the march. He had chosen the landing site and the direction of march with careful attention so there was very little chance of running into enemy troops or loyalists. They skirted towns and of course stayed off the main roads.

By midnight they had marched more than half of the journey. They stopped to rest before the final push on to Fort St. George. In this area of the Island they felt safe enough to light small cooking fires. Each man had nourishing food. The hot coffee was especially welcome. Tallmadge did not let them rest too long. He sensed they were sharply honed and ready for battle. Too much rest would reduce that fine edge. He pushed the men southward again.

The sun had not yet begun to rise when Tallmadge called a halt. They were now less than a mile from the fortifications of Fort St. George. They left their provisions and readied themselves for battle. As the dragoons and whaleboatmen checked their weapons, gunpowder, and shot, Major Tallmadge reviewed the plan of attack with Captain Edgar and Captain Brewster.

"Just as a review and to clarify; Captain Edgar and I will leave first so that we can circle around to the far side of the fort. We'll take two-thirds of the men. Once around the fort we'll split again so we can attack from two different locations. You, Cale, with the balance of the men, will attack from this side. The assault will begin as the first rays of sunrise hit the walls of the fort. Elijah, I leave you in charge of the dragoons who will go with Captain Brewster, but remember that he's your superior and you'll obey him as you would me. Is that understood?"

"Yes, sir, Major Tallmadge."

"Don't worry, Ben. I'll look after the boy," said Cale.

Elijah and Caleb watched as the first and larger group moved out in the dim pre-dawn light. Thick fog swirled about them as they pushed through it and disappeared in a blurry haze. Only minutes later Brewster called to the remaining men.

"Ready yourselves to move out." The men got to their feet and with very little talking, adjusting their gear. One dragoon reached for his musket which was leaning against a tree. It slipped from his grasp, fell to the ground, and discharged. The sound was startling and the men froze in their movements and listened for sounds from the fort.

"If they heard it, from this distance they'll think that it's just a hunter," said Cale. All eyes were upon him as he clutched at his left shoulder and then fell to the ground. The men stared at Brewster in disbelief. The invincible had fallen. Elijah was the first to reach him.

"Cale, Cale, what is it," said Elijah not wanting to believe that his friend had been hit by the musket shot. Caleb lifted his hand and Elijah saw blood oozing from a gaping wound.

"Cale, that musket shot ripped into you."

"Yes, boy, I've been hit. Damn! Damn the luck! Come on, boy, help me up. We got to move out now."

"You can't go anywhere. You're losing a lot of blood!"

"Don't tell me 'can't', boy. I've got to. The major is expec . . . " Brewster fell back mid-sentence. Elijah and two of Brewster's men reached out and grabbed him. They lowered him gently to the ground.

"Maybe you're right, boy. But you must go and go now. You've got to lead them, boy."

"Damn you, Cale. Stop calling me 'Boy'. I may be young, but I'm just as much a man as —"

"Then prove it! Ben needs you now. Forget me. Go. You know the plan of attack as well as I do. Go!"

Elijah looked at his friend and knew that he was right.

"I'll stay with him, Sergeant," said George Smith, one of the whaleboat men. "I'll see to him."

Elijah stood and without taking his eyes off Caleb Brewster said, "Third platoon, get ready to move out."

"That's it, b . . . ," said Brewster. "Go get'em and prove it!"

Elijah moved toward the head of the troop and ordered them to move out.

*

Elijah and his men had been on the move for just a few minutes when they met Major Tallmadge returning on the trail with his pistol in his hand. It was obvious that he'd been running at top speed. He was winded, agitated, and alarmed. Sighting the small troop he stopped and waited for them. Elijah called for a halt and went to Tallmadge.

"I heard a shot. What happened?"

"A musket accidentally discharged. Cale was wounded."

"Badly?"

"I couldn't tell. He's lost a lot of blood. Smith's with him. I had to go on without him."

"The only thing you could do. We'll go back for him later, but now we must move quickly to get these men into position. It's almost dawn."

The small band of soldiers approached the fort slowly and silently. The land immediately surrounding the fort had been cleared of trees and shrubbery, and this morning, a ground-hugging fog was thick and clung to the ground. Surrounding the fort was a ditch about four feet deep which would afford them some protection, but the men would have to crawl to the ditch first. They dropped to the ground and submerged in the fog. Every so often a man would poke his head above the thick ground fog to assure himself of direction. After reaching the trench, they examined the fortifications. A barricade of sharpened pickets and spikes were angled at the top of the ditch. Beyond the excavation and the sharp spikes was a formidable twelve foot stockade. The dragoons and whaleboatmen crawled slowly through the ditch. Each of the men loosened the spikes nearest them so they could easily be knocked aside when they scrambled out to attack the fort.

In the dim haze of the fog and early morning light, Major Tallmadge and Elijah could make out the figure of a lone Redcoat sentry pacing at the top of the stockade. Elijah pointed at the sentry and in a low hushed whisper spoke to Tallmadge.

"If he sees us and gives an alarm ... "

"Yes, and look, Elijah, the gate is opened. That's a break for us, but if he gives an alarm the first thing they'll do is close the gate," said Tallmadge in the same breathy voice. If we try to get to the gate we'll be seen. He paces just above that gate."

"I'll creep over to the gate and make sure it stays open," said Elijah crawling on his belly, quickly moving up and out of the ditch with his bayonet in his hand. He could hear Major Tallmadge's whispered voice behind him. "Elijah, no!" He thought of his mother and her tearful whisper as she also said "Elijah, no!" He thought of Cale Brewster, wounded and perhaps dying. William Tallmadge and Nathan Hale came to mind and he knew that it was now his turn to do what had to be done for freedom in this beautiful young country. Would he die as they did?

The first glimmer of light from the east began to show. In a moment the brilliance of the morning sun would illuminate the stockade walls and the attack would begin. He must get to that gate and keep it open at all costs. He continued to crawl toward the gate. He watched the sentry. When the sentry stopped, he stopped; afraid to breathe. He pressed himself closer to the ground. He could smell the rich damp earth. The guard peered over the wall and leaned forward trying to cut through the fog by squinting his eyes.

Elijah froze rigid to the ground keeping his eyes on the sentry. He felt totally exposed and vulnerable as the fog began to thin out. He could now see things in less of a haze. Could the sentry see him? If not now, how soon? Will his next feeling be a musket ball through his body? The sentry strained his eyes and peered directly at Elijah. He had to make out his form now. The sentry raised his rifle and aimed in his direction. Had he been seen? The rifle was pointed directly at his head. Elijah was not going to take that chance. If he was going to die, then he would die, but not lying on the ground like a target. He leaped to his feet and charged the stockade.

"Who goes there?" the sentry called out and fired his musket. Elijah heard the musket ball whistle pass him just inches from his ear. He reached the wall and climbed rapidly using the crossbars and rope lashings. Before the smoke from the guard's musket had cleared, Elijah had scaled the wall and was upon him. He grappled with the guard for a moment and then dispensed him with a quick movement of his bayonet. As the first rays of sunlight touched the fort, Elijah, brandishing his weapon above his head, shouted from the top of the stockade. "For Washington and Glory!" The attack had started.

Leaping with a yell from the wall into the fort, Elijah ran through the confused and disoriented Redcoats to the front gate. Two Redcoats were beginning to close the gate. Elijah slammed into them hard knocking them to the ground. He grasped the gate and pulled it open wider than before. A moment later, Major Tallmadge and his men charged through the now wide open gate.

Tallmadge tossed Elijah his musket. The two smiled at each other and charged into the fury of the battle. Another section of the wall had been breached and the second platoon of the American fighting force entered the fort.

There was more hand to hand fighting than Elijah had expected. He fired his musket once and had no time to reload as the Redcoats, like a sea of red ants, swarmed out of the barracks. The Redcoats fired a volley of shots at them and Elijah felt one sting as it tore the flesh of his shoulder. The enemy also had no time to reload and each side relied upon their bayonets. Lieutenant Kanfert had reached the top of the stockade. He and his men were firing upon the Redcoats. They knew that they had been bettered and they quickly surrendered. The battle was furious but short. Fort St. George was captured.

As prearranged, the American raiders destroyed the fortifications. The prisoners were made to carry the valuable munitions. The British also had horses which the dragoons readily took, happy to be back on horseback. Major Tallmadge sent a detachment of twelve dragoons, under the command of Captain Edgar, to sack the British storage depot in Coram. Before leaving the fort his men set it on fire destroying the dry goods which were kept there in large quantities.

After the fort was ablaze Major Tallmadge looked about for Elijah. He was no where to be found.

"Lieutenant Kanfert, Have you seen Sergeant Churchill?"

"Why yes, sir, I did. He left on horseback when the fort was secured after the battle. He said that you'd know where . . . "

"Yes, Lieutenant, I do indeed know where he went. Thank you, Lieutenant. Move the men out. We'll return in the same direction from which we came so we can join up with Sergeant Churchill and Captain Brewster."

*

Elijah wanted to rig a large stretcher for Cale Brewster but the big man would not hear of it. "I'll take a horse, but I'll not be carried. As you can see, George here, fixed me just fine. Bleedin's stopped. I'm fine I tell you. Enough about me, you've been wounded. It looks like a nasty wound you got there, Elijah. Bandage this man well, George."

"Are you sure you're well enough to travel?" asked Elijah ignoring his own wound and the pain it was causing him.

"Yes, but enough now, enough about me. Tell me, do I call you "boy" or what?"

"After his heroics today," said Benjamin Tallmadge as he rode up to the men, "We should call him, "Sir.""

"Tell me. I want to hear all about it," said Cale.

"Are you well enough to travel? I'll tell you as we go."

"Well enough? If we had the time I'd have been in the battle. Talk to me! Tell me all about the attack on the fort and especially about Elijah's part. Tell me everything."

"He should get a medal," said Tallmadge.

"Hey, Ben, we both know that only officers get medals."

"Oh, please, Major and you too, Cale. I didn't do anything special. I'm not a hero and I don't deserve a medal. I don't want to hear anymore about it."

NINETEEN

He had never experienced nor expected anything like this. Crowds of people lined the streets, cheering, applauding, and waving banners of red, white, and blue. In abundance were the flags of the new nation and people of all ages were waving them. Major Benjamin Tallmadge, astride his gallant black charger, led two hundred and fifty of his mounted dragoons through the streets of New York. A treaty of peace between Great Britain and the United States of America was signed in Paris on September 3, 1783. The war was over. The United States was a free and independent nation.

Benjamin and his dragoons were hailed as conquering heroes and this was not his intention. True, his was the first of the American forces to enter the city, but his thoughts of being first was only for the protection of the New York agents of the Culper Spy ring. He had requested and received permission from General Washington to enter New York earlier than any other American troop, specifically for that purpose.

The happy crowds pressed in closer, reaching out to touch the dragoons as they moved through the crowded streets. Major Tallmadge ordered his men to tighten ranks in an effort to keep the people from stepping into the path of the horses.

As they rounded one corner a band began to play. It was basically brass, drums, and fife, but the music added to the gaiety. The spirits of the people and the dragoons were raised to new heights of happiness, for it was thrilling to be alive and to be an American.

Elijah could not contain himself. He laughed out loud and cheered with the most clamorous voice. The war was over and he was a part of this great moment. He had achieved his boyhood dream and been part of the great revolution. A new nation was born. His happiness spilled over and he bubbled with new life and excitement. A young teenage girl rocked back and forth from heel to toe keeping with the beat of the drum.

Happiness beamed from her pretty face. Her smile was infectious and her laughter contagious as all about her laughed and smiled with her. She carried two open burlap sacks of chopped ice in her arms. They were tied together with cloth and slung over her shoulders and around her neck. Her rocking motion caused the excess ice chips to fall into the roadside where they sparkled and gleamed like diamonds in the dust of the road.

"You're spilling your ice," Elijah shouted to her. She laughed and spun around sending more ice chips in showers to the ground about her. The crowd cheered her as she danced to the music as ice cascaded about her.

As much as he was enjoying it, Major Tallmadge ordered his men to double time and quickly brought them away from the crowds. He left his officers in charge of quartering his men and went ahead to the quarters that had been provided for him. Elijah, still in the position as aide to the major, went along with him.

*

That very afternoon he and Elijah sought out Robert Townsend. They found Robert in his rooms, packing his belongings.

"But, Robert, surely you'll stay until General Washington arrives?"

"No, I'm sorry, but I want none of this pomp. I don't want anyone to know that I was Samuel Culper Jr."

This acclamation startled Benjamin. He never thought that the Culpers would remain anonymous after the war. In his eyes they were all heroes and deserving of recognition and honor.

"But, sir, you deserve the honors, and the right to revel in the gaiety of the occasion," said Elijah. He started to continue, but Benjamin shook his head and motioned to him to be silent.

Tallmadge looked at his top secret agent. His appearance had greatly changed from the last time the two had met years ago. Not only had he lost weight, but he looked haggard. His eyes were sunken and had black rings around them from poor nourishment and lack of sleep. He appeared ill. No. He looked like a man who had no reason to live.

"Are you ill?"

"Truly, I am, but it's a sickness of the heart and soul. I cannot rejoice as others might.

I've lost too much."

"I don't understand. Enlighten me, my friend."

Robert looked at the Major standing before him, the man he recognized now as John Bolton, leader of the Culper Spy ring. He certainly deserved an answer. He looked at Elijah and knew him also as a man who could be trusted. He motioned them both to a small table by the window. With weak and shaking hands he poured three glasses of rum. Tallmadge raised his glass in a toast.

"To Washington and glory!"

"Yes, and to those who died for Washington and glory," added Townsend. The tone of his voice was bitter.

"To all those who died. Nathan Hale, my brother, William . . ."

"To agent 355," said Robert with a voice choked with emotion. The three men sipped their rum and sat in silence for a while. Tallmadge waited for Townsend to compose himself. When he did, Tallmadge said, "Tell me about agent 355."

"She died for the Culper Ring, what more do you want to know?"

"I know nothing about agent 355. I didn't even know the agent was a woman. What was she like? Tell me of her, please . . . if you will?"

Fortifying himself with another drink of rum, he began, "Did you know that I was a Quaker? No? . . . well no, I don't suppose you did. How would you know? Well, I am, or at least I was. It goes against my beliefs to lie and be deceitful, yet that's the nature of being a spy. I did that for you. Not happily, but I did it." His face became streaked with tears which he made no effort to hide or even wipe away. He continued. "It went against my beliefs, against my very soul and nature as a man to dress like an English dandy. I did that for you as well. I used people to gain information. I did that for you, too. I began to hate myself and I sunk into periods of great despair. Then one day I met . . . Agent 355.

"She eventually volunteered to be a spy. For me. That she did . . . for me! And I used her and . . . then, . . . and then . . . I fell in love with her. She wouldn't quit spying for us, the Culpers, no matter how much I begged her. And then, one day information that I, . . . that I," he pounded his chest with a frail hand and sobbed. "Information that I gave to the Ring led to a sweep of all possible spies. She was captured, because of me. She . . . died aboard that damn prison ship the *Jersey*. I could not save her."

Robert Townsend's eyes glazed over and he wept openly. After a moment Tallmadge asked, "What was her name?"

"355," Townsend slowly answered.

"Not her code number. Tell me her name so that she may be properly honored."

"355," repeated Townsend, his jaw set with determination. "She needs no honors. She lives in my heart and that's where her name will stay, forever!"

"Forgive me, Robert. I'll intrude no longer."

"No, dear friend, it's I who should beg your forgiveness. Thank you for coming to me. Thank you for caring, but I wish no honors. I wish to remain anonymous. I ask for your promise. From both of you."

"You have my word."

"And mine, sir," said Elijah.

"Then it is done. I know you both to be honorable men. I'd ask you both to leave me now. I wish to leave New York as soon as possible."

Major Tallmadge and Elijah stood and made their farewells. At the doorway, Tallmadge turned to Robert and said, "Good-bye, Robert. Thanking you seems so inadequate. This country owes you so much. I pray that God grants you the peace you seek."

TWENTY

Major Tallmadge entered the tavern to the cheers of his dragoons. He made his way through the boisterous crowd amid clasps on the back and handshakes. Elijah moved right along behind him and with the assistance of others hoisted the major up on their shoulders. Once all could see him the cheering became even louder. One group of dragoons broke out into a song of praise that soon all were singing.

They carried him to the center of the tavern and stood him on a table. Although he raised his arms to quiet them, they continued cheering and singing. There was no stopping their boisterous enthusiasm. They handed him a large stein of ale and he joined in on the camaraderie. He sang their praises and applauded them and then again tried to get their attention. Finally in desperation he shouted, "Attention!"

The crowd quickly quieted down as most of the startled dragoons snapped to attention. The other quickly followed suit. All thought that perhaps a higher ranking officer had entered. Benjamin looked about at the silent startled group of faithful followers and smiled.

"Gentlemen, please, forgive the rouse. As you were, but please, I wish a moment of your attention. I've something to say. I don't wish to interrupt your merriment, but we soon will be going our separate ways and I cannot let you go without . . . well . . . without speaking to you about how I feel."

Once again he slowly glanced around the tavern from his lofty perch on the table. His eyes lingered on one soldier or another. He smiled and nodded to them as he tried to compose himself and find the proper words to express his feelings. The dragoons knew what he was about. They shared his feelings of love and pride in their regiment. A few took a deep breath as they waited for their leader to speak. Others found it difficult to swallow the large lump of emotion that they suddenly found in their throat.

"My fellow comrades-at-arms, my friends. We've come through quite a lot together. All of us have shared a portion of our lives which will join us for eternity. In our revelry today let us not forget to lift our glasses high to those fallen friends and brothers who will forever be in our hearts. You cheer me. You lift me on your shoulders. I thank you for the honor. I accept this for the regiment, but I come here to thank you and to praise you. No officer has ever commanded a finer group of fighting men. I feel that I know you all quite well. Some more than others and some," he glanced at Elijah, "some I feel that I've raised as a son."

All knew that he spoke of Elijah and all including Elijah laughed as Tallmadge joked. Speaking directly to Elijah, he continued, "I've know you since you were, what was it? Thirteen? Fourteen? I'm as proud of you as if I were your father. I'm too young to be your father, but we're truly brothers. As we all are joined as a family, we've been fathers and brothers to each other. As we go our separate ways, we'll keep each other eternally in our hearts. To your glasses gentlemen. I drink to you all. I drink to the finest regiment of dragoons, finer than any man could ever hope to lead. I drink to each and every one of you. May God be with you all the days of your life."

Tallmadge lifted his stein and said, "Gentleman, one final toast. Words that have seemed to guide us through all these long years. To Washington and Glory!"

"To Washington and Glory," shouted the men in unison.

"God bless our major," said one of the dragoons. The cheering and singing started all over again as Tallmadge leaped from the table and putting his arm around Elijah, led him from the tavern.

"Why are we leaving?" asked Elijah.

"I have to be at another tavern today. General Washington has asked all of the officers to meet with him."

"I'm not an officer. Can't I stay with the regiment? It's not right for me to be where the officers are."

"Ha! That never stopped you before. I want you there with me. Don't question me, Elijah. You're still in the army, you know."

"Yes, sir," said Elijah reluctantly.

The two dragoons walked the streets in silence. The major stole a glance or two at the sergeant who was not at all pleased to be going to an officer's meeting. Before long they entered Fraunces' Tavern. Just inside the door Benjamin turned to Elijah.

"Elijah, stand here and guard."

"Yes, sir, but guard what, sir?"

"Just guard, Elijah, just guard," he said smiling.

"Do I guard against those coming in or those coming out?"

"Both. If they are coming in you say 'Hello' and if they are going out you say 'Good-bye'. Understood?" said Tallmadge continuing in his jovial manner.

"Yes, sir . . . but . . . "

"Understood?"

"Yes, sir."

Fraunces' Tavern was a large establishment with many meeting rooms. The tavern also had the facilities to accommodate guests. It was here that General Washington had established lodging and here that he had called a meeting of his officers.

Major Tallmadge entered a large meeting hall behind the main tap room. Here many of his dragoons had already entered by the back door and other were still filing in. Their faces all had smiles which were more like smirks. They formed themselves in ranks at attention on the one side of the room which was devoid of furniture. Through the center door entered many high ranking officers. The dragoons snapped rigidly and smartly to attention. Major Tallmadge saluted as general after general entered the room. General Washington was the last to enter and the room was in a hushed silence. The tall austere gentleman general approached Benjamin. Smiling, he opened an ornate box. He removed a medal and showed it to Benjamin.

"How do you like it, Benjamin?"

"It's beautiful, sir. I've never seen anything quite like it."

"I'm surprised, for it was you who gave me the idea."

"I, sir?"

"Yes, Benjamin. You once described the jacket of a slain private. A musket ball had ripped the cloth and the infantryman's blood had stained it purple. Do you remember? It was quite some time ago."

"Yes, sir, I do remember."

"That's why this medal is made of purple silk and edged in silver binding. The laurel leaves on the top and bottom are my idea. If my memory serves me correctly, it was Churchill who wore that uniform. Am I right?"

"Yes, sir. He took it from a dead private on the battle field who had been shot through the heart. Elijah said on that very night that he would do nothing to dishonor that uniform and he hasn't."

"Before we continue, I want you to know that my gratitude knows no bounds where you are concerned. Your success with gathering intelligence was eminently more important to our victory than you can ever imagine. I've recommended to the

Continental Congress that if they ever wanted an agency to centralize the gathering of intelligence, they should call upon your skills, and use your secret service."

"I'll always be happy to serve my country in any way the Congress sees fit."

"Well, let's get our man in here, Lieutenant Colonel Tallmadge."

"Sir?" said the startled new Lieutenant Colonel. "I don't know what to say."

"This is a day full of surprises, isn't it, Benjamin? Don't look so overwhelmed. You deserve it. Now get that sergeant in here."

Benjamin went to the door and called out to Elijah. "Elijah, will you come in here, please?"

"Yes, sir, Major Tallmadge."

Elijah entered the room and was stunned by the array of high ranking officers all smiling and looking at him. He looked over and saw his regiment of dragoons smiling as well and standing at attention.

"Should I fall in with the others, sir? Oh, my God, isn't that General Washington?" said Elijah in a hushed voice.

"Yes, Sergeant, just follow me."

Tallmadge marched directly to General Washington with Elijah following. Elijah's eyes were flashing with trepidation, uncertainty, and wonderment.

"General Washington, sir. I have the distinct pleasure of presenting Sergeant Elijah Churchill," said Benjamin with unmistakable pride.

"It has been said," began the general, "that only the officers get the medals, but the officers know that behind their medals from victory in this battle or that, are the many unselfish deeds of heroism by men of valor who do not happen to be officers. It is truly so in this case. In many battles and in particular the battle of Fort St. George, Sergeant Elijah Churchill of the Second Regiment of Light Dragoons, showed great gallantry in the face of danger to his person, showed firmness and address in the surprise attack on the fort. He was also wounded in this battle. His officers tell me that success was largely due to an overwhelming act of bravery by Sergeant Churchill. Elijah, I have personally designed this medal. I pin it upon your chest with the respect of a grateful nation. And, Sergeant Elijah Churchill, please accept my hand with the respect of a grateful fellow soldier."

Elijah and the general shook hands and Benjamin was glad he didn't have to speak because of the emotional pride which welled up within him making speech impossible.

General Washington left the room followed by the other officers. The dragoons let out a war whoop and swarmed around Elijah and now it was his turn to be lifted in the air. They carried him off, presumably back to the first tavern. Benjamin Tallmadge watched as his regiment left the room, then he turned and left the meeting room and joined General Washington and the other officers.

*

The officers were enjoying a refreshing light wine when General Washington entered the room. He too filled his glass with wine. The room was consumed with an unnatural stillness as each of the officers watched their commander-in-chief. He walked to the windows, sipped his wine and walked back to a large desk. Slowly placing his wine glass down he turned to the gathered officers. He spoke quietly and slowly almost as if he didn't want to utter the words.

"With a heart filled with love and gratitude, I now take my leave of you. I most devoutly wish that your latter days may be as prosperous and happy as your former ones have been glorious and honorable."

He stopped for a moment as if gathering his words and to control his emotion. He lifted his wine glass from the table and without drinking, replaced it. The stillness in the room prevailed as the officers waited for their general to continue.

"I cannot come to each of you, but shall feel obliged if each of you will come and take me by the hand."

The officers one by one went to their leader. They were all unable to speak and each was overcome with emotion. The general embraced each of them. No one spoke. No one could find a word to pierce the beauty of this silent tribute paid to the man who had led them and their nation to freedom.

General Washington left the room followed by his attending officers. He greeted his family and slowly walked between guards of light infantry who lined the way to the barge which waited for him. Not a word was spoken. As his barge pulled away he stood up and faced them. He returned their warmest salute with a simple wave of his hat.

TWENTY ONE

The December morning had a stillness about it, a feeling that snow was imminent, but the sky was clear and the sun began to rise spreading color and the promise of an unusually warm day. Benjamin Tallmadge and Elijah saddled their horses in the old stable behind Townsend & Company. Austin Roe was already mounted on his favorite mare who pawed at the ground in anticipation of the morning ride.

"I've been making this ride for years, but this is the first time that I'll have anyone come along with me. Are you sure that you want to do this? It would be easier by coach," said Roe.

"No thank you, Austin. This is the only aspect of the Ring that I've not experienced. I want to make my feeling complete. I want to travel the courier's route," said Benjamin.

"It's a funny feeling, going home after being away for so long. I don't know if I'll be welcome. I'm glad to have someone to ride with me. And, remember, Maj . . . er . . . Colonel, you promised to come to my home with me," said Elijah.

"I'll keep my word. I'd like to meet your family, Elijah," said Benjamin as he mounted his big Black.

"I hope I still have a family," said Elijah climbing on to his mare. "I didn't contact them, not once."

"They'll be proud of you."

"Let's go," said Austin.

"Let's make it a nice and easy ride. We're not carrying any express messages today."

The three men laughed as they turned their horses into the road that would take them to the Brooklyn ferry. Along the way Austin pointed out places where incidents had taken place. Some of the incidents had been frightening occurrences when Austin had been fearful of discovery. Today was different of course, and they laughed as Austin made light of his danger at the time.

They enjoyed a light lunch at an Inn in Hampstead. This was a pleasure that Roe had little time for on past journeys. By mid-afternoon the three riders approached the farm of Abraham Woodhull. As they rode up, Abraham came out of the farmhouse to greet them.

"My, my. What a pleasure to see the three of you together. And don't you two look splendid in your uniforms. I see that you are now a Colonel. It's now Colonel Tallmadge."

"The war is over, Abraham. Call me Ben."

Neither of the men saw a giant of a man come around the farmhouse. He came up behind them and lifted Elijah off his horse.

"Cale! Cale, you bull! Put me down," yelled Elijah.

"How are you Cale? But I can see that you are fully recovered from your wound," said Benjamin.

"Fully recovered and raring to go. Any wars brewing that we can get into?"

"Haven't you had your fill of fighting?" asked Elijah as the big man set him on his feet.

"Oh, I've done enough resting and besides, I promised too many women that I'd marry them after the war was over. So you see, gentlemen, a war could save my life."

The men enjoyed the laughter and all agreed that they couldn't see Caleb Brewster settled down.

"But," he continued, "I must consider the line of Brewsters, you know . . . "

"Yes we know," said Benjamin. "Please don't remind us."

Again they all laughed and were still laughing when they entered the house for a drink of rum. After about an hour, Austin Roe took his leave. That seemed to spur on the others and soon Benjamin and Elijah said their farewells.

"Abraham, what can I say that hasn't already been said in one way or another? Your services to this country have been immeasurable. If you ever need me, you have only to ask and I'll be ready."

"Thank you, Ben."

"Ben, I'll see you later on tonight. I'll be waiting at the dock in Setauket Bay at . . . What did we say? . . . 10 tonight?"

"Yes, Cale, 10 o'clock will be perfect. If the weather turns bad we can stay in town tonight and then go across to Connecticut in the morning," said Benjamin.

"The weather'll be just fine. I feel that it'll snow, but the Sound will be calm. See you later, Ben. Good-bye, Elijah. Don't forget me," said Caleb.

"Forget you? Who could forget you?"

With a wave the two dragoons set off down the road and set a pace that would bring them to the Churchill farm, as quickly as possible. Elijah was unusually quiet. On occasion he would look at the man who had been leader, friend, brother, and at times a father to him. He knew that they would be parting soon. He also knew that he would be facing his real father in a very short time.

The familiar road turned sharply and there before them was the Churchill farm. Elijah slowed his mare and the two horsemen continued up to the farmhouse. A young girl of thirteen or fourteen stared at them.

"Ma, there's two soldiers here," the girl called out.

The door swung open and Elijah's mother stepped out onto the porch. She was drying her hands on her apron as she steadied her eyes at the two men. Her attention went to Elijah who dismounted and approached her. He smiled and removing his white plumed helmet, he took a step toward her. She looked at him and tears burst forth from her eyes.

"Ma," said Elijah, his own eyes infused with tears.

"Elijah? It's really you? Elijah, Elijah my son! I'd almost given up all hope."

Mother and son fell into each other's arms. They separated only to look at each other as each was incapable of speech. Finally Elijah was able to introduce his fellow traveler.

"Mother, this is Colonel Benjamin Tallmadge."

She nodded at Benjamin as she took Elijah by the arm.

"I'm indeed pleased to meet you, Colonel. You're welcome here. Please come inside. My husband would be happy to see you as well."

They entered the farmhouse and Benjamin and Elijah could see a man by the stone fireplace. He was tapping the remnants of his pipe tobacco out into the fire. The older man turned and father and son stood face to face once again. Neither spoke at first, and Elijah was immobile. He studied his father's weather-worn face. The elder Churchill swallowed hard and started to shake a little as he could no longer contain his emotion. He embraced his son and held him tightly.

"Father, when last we spoke . . . "

"No more of that. That was then and this is now. I'm proud of you, my son."

"And you have a son to be very proud of indeed," said Benjamin.

"Father, this is Colonel Benjamin Tallmadge of the . . . "

"I know who he is, son. The whole country knows about Ben. His exploits and fame have preceeded him."

"Your son was with me through all of it, sir. That medal on his chest is the first of its kind. Awarded for heroic bravery and wounds received in battle. General Washington designed it and awarded it to Elijah personally. The general calls it . . . . The Purple Heart."

*

Some hours later Benjamin Tallmadge left the farmhouse. He and Elijah said tentative good-byes. At first they shook hands and then embraced as brothers. Benjamin mounted his horse and rode off toward the bay. He stopped just outside the farm and looked back. He could see Elijah on the porch waving to him.

A soft snow had begun to fall upon the cold ground. Soon all of Long Island would be blanketed with a covering of pure white beauty. The snow would cover the ruts and grooves caused by the heavy British wagons and cannons. The marks of horses hooves and British Cavalry boots would be covered as well. Would the pain and anguish of loss caused by war be covered as easily? Like the snow, the pure pristine mantel of freedom gave hope for a glorious future in the sweet land of liberty.